The Darkness

Ragnar Jónasson was born in Reykjavík, Iceland, where he works as a writer and a lawyer, and also teaches copyright law at Reykjavík University. He has previously worked on radio and television, including as a TV news reporter for the Icelandic National Broadcasting Service, and has translated fourteen of Agatha Christie's novels from the age of seventeen. He is an international number one bestseller.

The Darkness is the first novel in his Hidden Iceland series, to be followed by *The Island* and *The Mist*.

The Darkness

RAGNAR JÓNASSON

Translated from the Icelandic
by Victoria Cribb

MICHAEL JOSEPH
an imprint of
PENGUIN BOOKS

MICHAEL JOSEPH

UK | USA | Canada | Ireland | Australia
India | New Zealand | South Africa

Michael Joseph is part of the Penguin Random House group of companies
whose addresses can be found at global.penguinrandomhouse.com

First published in Iceland with the title *Dimma* by Veröld Publishing 2015
First published in Great Britain by Michael Joseph 2018
001

Copyright © Ragnar Jónasson, 2015
English translation copyright © Victoria Cribb, 2018

The moral right of the author and translator has been asserted

Set in 13.75/16.25 pt Garamond MT Std
Typeset by Jouve (UK), Milton Keynes
Printed in Great Britain by Clays Ltd, St Ives plc

A CIP catalogue record for this book is available from the British Library

HARDBACK ISBN: 978–0–718–18724–8
OM PAPERBACK ISBN: 978–0–718–18781–1

www.greenpenguin.co.uk

To my mother

Special thanks are due to Haukur Eggertsson for his advice on expeditions to the highlands and interior, and to prosecutor Hulda María Stefánsdóttir for her assistance with police procedure.

'Rage, like a bolt from hell, twists all a man's limbs, kindles an inferno in his eyes . . .'

Bishop Jón Vídalín

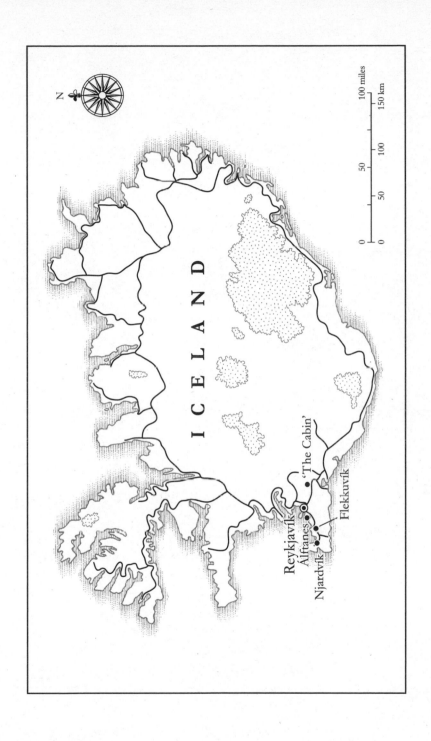

Day One

I

'How did you find me?' the woman asked. There was a tremor in her voice; her face was frightened.

Detective Inspector Hulda Hermannsdóttir felt her interest quicken, though as an old hand at this game she had learned to expect a nervous reaction from those she interviewed, even when they had nothing to hide. Being questioned by the police was an intimidating business at any time, whether it was a formal interview down at the station or an informal chat like this one. They sat facing one another in a poky coffee room next to the staff canteen at the Reykjavík nursing home where the woman worked. She was around forty, with short-cropped hair, tired-looking, apparently flustered by Hulda's unexpected visit. Of course, there could be a perfectly innocent explanation for this, but Hulda was almost sure the woman had something to hide. Over the years she had spoken to so many suspects she had developed a knack of spotting when people were trying to pull the wool over her eyes. Some might have called it intuition, but Hulda despised the word, regarding it as a sign of lazy policing.

'How did I find you . . . ?' she repeated calmly. 'Didn't you want to be found?' This was twisting the woman's words, but she had to get the conversation going somehow.

'What? Yes . . .'

There was a taint of coffee in the air – you couldn't call it an aroma – and the cramped room was dark, the furniture dated and drably institutional.

The woman had her hand on the table. When she raised it to her cheek again, it left a damp print behind. Normally, Hulda would have been pleased by this telltale sign that she had found her culprit, but she felt none of the usual satisfaction.

'I need to ask you about an incident that took place last week,' Hulda continued after a brief pause. As was her habit, she spoke a little fast, her voice friendly and upbeat, part of the positive persona she had adopted in her professional life, even when performing difficult tasks like the present one. Alone at home in the evenings, she could be the complete opposite of this person, all her reserves of energy depleted, leaving her prey to tiredness and depression.

The woman nodded: clearly, she knew what was coming next.

'Where were you on Friday morning?'

The answer came straight back: 'At work, as far as I remember.'

Hulda felt almost relieved that the woman wasn't going

to give up her freedom without a fight. 'Are you sure about that?' she asked. Watching intently for the woman's reaction, she leaned back in her chair, arms folded, in her usual interviewing pose. Some would take this as a sign that she was on the defensive or lacked empathy. On the defensive? As if. It was simply to stop her hands from getting in the way and distracting her when she needed to focus. As for lacking empathy, she felt no need to engage her emotions any more than she already did naturally: her job took quite enough of a toll on her. She pursued her inquiries with integrity and a level of dedication that, she knew, bordered on the obsessive.

'Are you sure?' she repeated. 'We can easily check up on that. You wouldn't want to be caught out in a lie.'

The woman said nothing, but her discomfort was plain.

'A man was hit by a car,' Hulda said, matter-of-factly.

'Oh?'

'Yes, you must have seen it in the papers or on TV.'

'What? Oh, maybe.' After a short silence, the woman added: 'How is he?'

'He'll survive, if that's what you're fishing for.'

'No, not really . . . I . . .'

'But he'll never make a full recovery. He's still in a coma. So you are aware of the incident?'

'I . . . I must have read about it . . .'

'It wasn't reported in the papers, but the man was a convicted paedophile.'

When the woman didn't react, Hulda went on: 'But you must have known that when you knocked him down.'

Still no reaction.

'He was given a prison sentence years ago and had done his time.'

The woman interrupted: 'What makes you think I had anything to do with it?'

'Like I was saying, he'd done his time. But, as we discovered during the investigation, that didn't mean he'd stopped. You see, we had reason to believe the hit-and-run wasn't an accident, so we searched his flat to try and work out a possible motive. That's when we found all these pictures.'

'Pictures?' The woman was looking badly shaken now. 'What of?' She held her breath.

'Children.'

The woman was obviously desperate to ask more but wouldn't let herself.

'Including your son,' Hulda added, in reply to the question that had not been asked.

Tears began to slide down the woman's face. 'Pictures . . . of my son,' she stammered, her breath catching on a sob.

'Why didn't you report him?' Hulda asked, trying not to make it sound like an accusation.

'What? I don't know. Of course, I should have done . . . But I was thinking of him, you see. Thinking of my son. I couldn't bear to do that to him. He'd have had to . . . tell people . . . testify in court. Maybe it was a mistake . . .'

'To run the man down? Yes, it was.'

After a slight hesitation, the woman went on: 'Well . . . yes . . . but . . .'

Hulda waited, allowing a space to develop for the woman's confession. Yet she wasn't experiencing any of her usual sense of achievement at solving the crime. Usually, she focused on excelling at her job, and prided herself on the number of difficult cases she had solved over the years. The trouble now was that she wasn't at all convinced the woman sitting in front of her was the real culprit in this case, despite her guilt. If anything, she was the victim.

Sobbing uncontrollably now, the woman said: 'I ... I watched ...' then broke off, too choked up to continue.

'You watched him? You live in the same area, don't you?'

'Yes,' the woman whispered, getting her voice under control, anger lending her a sudden strength. 'I kept an eye on the bastard. I couldn't bear the idea that he might carry on doing those things. I kept waking up with nightmares, dreaming that he'd chosen another victim. And ... and ... it was all my fault because I hadn't reported him. You see?'

Hulda nodded. She saw, all right.

'Then I spotted him, by the school. I'd just given my son a lift in. I parked the car and watched him – he was chatting to some boys, with that ... that disgusting smirk on his face. He hung around the playground for a while and I got so angry. He hadn't stopped – men like him, they never do.' She wiped her cheeks, but the tears kept pouring down her face.

'Quite.'

'Then, out of the blue, I got my chance. When he left

the school, I followed him. He crossed the road. There was no one else around, no one to see me, so I just put my foot down. I don't know what I was thinking – I wasn't really thinking at all.' The woman broke into loud sobbing again and buried her face in her hands, before continuing, shakily: 'I didn't mean to kill him, or I don't think I did. I was just frightened and angry. What'll happen to me now? I can't . . . I can't go to prison. There's only the two of us, my son and me. His father's useless. There's no way he'll take him.'

Without a word, Hulda stood up and laid a hand on the woman's shoulder.

II

The young mother stood by the glass and waited. As usual, she had dressed up for the visit. Her best coat was looking a little shabby, but money was tight so it would have to do. They always made her wait, as if to punish her, to remind her of her mistake and give her a chance to reflect on the error of her ways. To make matters worse, it had been raining outside and her coat was damp.

Several minutes passed in what felt like an eternity of silence before a nurse finally entered the room carrying the little girl. The mother's heart turned over, as it always did when she saw her daughter through the glass. She felt overwhelmed by a wave of depression and despair but made a valiant effort to hide it. Though the child was only six months old – today, in fact – and unlikely to remember anything about the visit, her mother felt instinctively that it was vital any memories she did have were positive, that these visits should be happy occasions.

But the child looked far from happy and, what was

worse, showed almost no reaction to the woman on the other side of the glass. She might have been looking at a stranger: an odd woman in a damp coat who she'd never laid eyes on before. Yet it wasn't that long since she had been lying in her mother's arms in the maternity ward.

The woman was permitted two visits a week. It wasn't enough. Every time she came she sensed the distance between them widening: only two visits a week and a sheet of glass between them.

The mother tried to say something to her daughter; tried to speak through the glass. She knew the sound would carry, but what good would the words do? The little girl was too young to understand: what she needed was to be cradled in her mother's arms.

Fighting back her tears, the woman smiled at her daughter, telling her in a low voice how much she loved her. 'Make sure you eat enough,' she said. 'Be a good girl for the nurses.' When really all she wanted was to smash the glass and snatch her baby from the nurse's arms, to hold her tight and never let her go again.

Without realizing it, she had moved right up to the glass. She tapped it gently and the little girl's mouth twitched in a slight smile that melted her mother's heart. The first tear spilled over and trickled down her cheek. She tapped a little louder, but the child flinched and started to cry as well.

Unable to help herself, the mother started banging louder and louder on the glass, shouting: 'Give her to me, I want my daughter!'

The nurse got up and hurriedly left the room with the

baby, but even then the mother couldn't stop her banging and shouting.

Suddenly, she felt a firm hand on her shoulder. She stopped beating at the glass and looked around at the older woman who was standing behind her. They had met before.

'Now, you know this won't do,' the woman said gently. 'We can't let you visit if you make a fuss like this. You'll frighten your little girl.'

The words echoed in the mother's head. She'd heard it all before: that it was in the child's best interests not to form too close a bond with her mother; it would only make the wait between visits more difficult. She must understand that this arrangement was for her daughter's sake.

It made no sense at all to her, but she pretended to understand, terrified of being banned from visiting.

Outside in the rain again, she made up her mind that once they were reunited she would never tell her daughter about this time, about the glass and the enforced separation. She only hoped the little girl wouldn't remember.

III

It was getting on for six when Hulda finished questioning the woman, so she headed straight home. She needed time to think before taking the next step.

Summer was coming and the days were growing longer, but there was no sign of the sun, just rain and more rain.

In her memories, the summers had been warmer and brighter, bathed in sunshine. So many memories: too many, really. It was incredible to think she was about to turn sixty-five. She didn't feel as if her sixties were half over, as if seventy was looming on the horizon.

Accepting your age was one thing; accepting retirement quite another. But there was no getting away from it: all too soon, she would be drawing her pension. Not that she knew how someone her age was supposed to feel. Her mother had been an old woman at sixty, if not before, but now that it was Hulda's turn, she couldn't feel any real difference between being forty-four and sixty-four. Maybe she had a little less stamina these days, but not that you'd notice. Her eyesight was still pretty good, though her hearing wasn't quite what it used to be.

She kept herself fit, too: her love of the outdoors saw to that. Why, she even had a certificate to prove she wasn't an old woman. 'In excellent shape,' the young doctor had said – far too young to be a doctor, of course – at her last medical. Actually, what he'd said was: 'In excellent shape *for your age.*'

She'd kept her figure, and her short hair was still naturally dark, with only a few grey hairs here and there. It was only when she looked in the mirror that she noticed the ravages of time. Sometimes she couldn't believe her eyes, feeling as if the person reflected there was a stranger, someone she'd rather not recognize, though her face was familiar. The wrinkles here and there, the bags under her eyes, the sagging skin. Who was this woman, and what was she doing in Hulda's mirror?

She was sitting in the good armchair, her mother's chair, staring out of the living-room window. It wasn't much of a view; pretty much what you'd expect from the fourth floor of a city tower block.

It hadn't always been this way. Occasionally, she allowed herself a fleeting moment of nostalgia for the old days, for family life in their house by the sea on Álftanes. Allowed herself to remember. The birdsong had been so much louder and more persistent there; you only had to step out into the garden to be close to nature. Of course, the proximity to the sea had made it windy, but the fresh ocean air, cold though it was, had been a lifeline for Hulda. She used to stand on the shore below their house, close her eyes, fill her mind with the sounds of nature – the boom of the waves, the mewing of the gulls – and simply breathe.

The years had flown by so quickly. It hardly seemed any time since she had become a mother, since she had got married. But when she started counting the years, she realized it was a lifetime ago. Time was like a concertina: one minute compressed, the next stretching out interminably.

She knew she was going to miss her job, in spite of all the times she had felt aggrieved that her talents weren't appreciated. In spite of the glass ceiling she had so often found herself banging her head against.

The truth was that she dreaded being lonely, though there was a potential bright spot on the horizon. She still didn't know where her friendship with the man from the walking club was going, but the possibilities it opened up were both tantalizing and unsettling. She had been single, more or less, ever since becoming a widow and had done nothing to encourage the man's advances at first. She had kept dwelling on the disadvantages of the relationship and worrying about her age, which wasn't like her. Usually, she did her best to forget it; thought of herself as young at heart. But this time the number – sixty-four! – had got in the way. She kept asking herself if it was really a good idea to begin a new relationship at that age but soon realized this was nothing but an empty excuse for avoiding taking a risk. She was afraid, that was all.

Whatever happened, Hulda was determined to take it

slowly. There was no need to rush into anything. She liked him and could easily imagine spending her twilight years with him. It wasn't love – she'd forgotten what that felt like – but love wasn't a requirement for her. They shared a passion for the great outdoors, which wasn't to be taken for granted, and she enjoyed his company. But she knew there was another reason she had agreed to see him again after that first date. If she were honest, her impending retirement had been the deciding factor: she couldn't face the prospect of growing old alone.

IV

The email troubled Hulda, though the request seemed simple enough. Her boss wanted to meet her at nine that morning to talk things over. The email had been sent late the previous evening, which was unusual in itself, and it was most unlike him to want to start the day by 'talking things over' with *her*. Hulda was used to seeing him holding informal morning meetings, but she had never been invited to one herself. These weren't work meetings so much as bonding sessions for the boys, and she definitely wasn't part of that gang. Despite all her years in a position of responsibility, she still had the feeling that she didn't enjoy the full trust of her superiors – or of her juniors, for that matter. Management hadn't been able to overlook her entirely when it came to promotion but, eventually, she had hit a brick wall. The positions she applied for kept going to her younger, male colleagues, and in the end she had accepted the inevitable. Instead of applying for further laurels, she had settled for doing her job as a detective inspector as well as she could.

So it was with some trepidation that she went along the corridor to Magnús's office. He answered her knock promptly, affable as ever, but Hulda had the feeling his friendliness was all on the surface.

'Take a seat, Hulda,' he said, and she bristled at what she took to be a note of condescension in his voice, whether conscious or not.

'I've got a lot on,' she said. 'Is it important?'

'Take a seat,' he repeated. 'We need to have a little chat about your situation.' Magnús was in his early forties; he'd risen fast through the ranks of the police. He was tall and healthy looking, if unusually thin on top for a man his age.

She sat down, her heart sinking. Her situation?

'You haven't got long now,' Magnús began, smiling. When Hulda said nothing, he cleared his throat and tried again, a little more awkwardly: 'I mean, this is your last year with us, isn't it?'

'Yes, that's right,' she said hesitantly. 'I'm due to retire at the end of the year.'

'Exactly. The thing is . . .' He broke off, as if choosing his words with care: 'we've got a young man joining us next month. A real high achiever.'

Hulda still wasn't sure where this conversation was heading.

'He'll be taking over from you,' Magnús continued. 'We were extremely lucky to get him. He could have gone abroad or into the private sector.'

She felt as if she'd been punched in the stomach. 'What? Taking over from me? What . . . what do you mean?'

'He'll be taking over your job and your office.'

Hulda was speechless. The thoughts began racing around in her head. 'When?' she asked hoarsely, finding her voice again.

'In two weeks.'

'But . . . but what'll happen to me?' She felt floored by the news.

'You can go now, straight away. You don't have much time left anyway. It's only a question of bringing your leaving date forward by a few months.'

'Leave? Straight away?'

'Yes. On full pay, of course. You're not being sacked, Hulda, you'll just be taking a few months' leave, then you'll continue straight on to your pension. It won't affect the amount you receive. There's no need to look so surprised. It's a good deal. I'm not trying to short-change you.'

'A good deal?'

'Of course. It'll give you more time for your hobbies. More time for . . .' His expression betrayed the fact that he had no idea what she got up to in her leisure time. 'More time to spend with . . .' Again, he trailed off midsentence: he should have known that Hulda had no family.

'It's kind of you to offer, but I don't want to retire early,' Hulda said stiffly, trying to control her expression. 'Thanks, all the same.'

'It wasn't an offer, actually: I've already made my decision.' Magnús's voice had taken on a harder edge.

'Your decision? Don't I get any say?'

'I'm sorry, Hulda. We need your office.'

And to surround yourself with a younger team, she thought.

'Is that all the thanks I get?' She could hear the wobble in her voice.

'Now, don't take it so badly. It's not intended as any reflection on your abilities. Come on, Hulda: you know you're one of the best officers we've got – we both know that.'

'But what about my caseload?'

'I've already allocated most of it to other members of the team. Before you leave, you can sit down with the new guy and put him in the picture. The biggest thing you're handling at the moment is the hit-and-run on the paedophile. Have you made any progress there?'

She thought for a moment. It would have been satisfying to her ego to end on a high note: case closed, confession in the bag. A woman who had, in a moment of madness, taken the law into her own hands to prevent further children from falling into the clutches of an abuser. Perhaps there had been a kind of justice in the attack, a just revenge . . .

'I'm nowhere near solving that one, I'm afraid,' she said after a pause. 'If you ask me, it was probably an accident. I'd advise shelving the case for the time being and hoping the driver will come forward in due course.'

'Hmm, right. OK, fine. We'll hold a little reception to give you a formal send-off later this year, when you officially retire. But you can clear your desk today, if you like.'

'You want me to leave . . . today?'

'Sure, if you like. Or you can stay another couple of weeks, if you'd prefer.'

'Yes, please,' she said, immediately regretting the 'please'. 'I'll leave when the new man starts, but until then I'll continue working on my cases.'

'Like I said, they've all been reallocated. But you, well, you could always look into a cold case, I suppose. Anything that takes your fancy. How does that grab you?'

She felt a momentary impulse to jump up and storm out, never to return, but she wasn't going to give him the satisfaction.

'Fine, I'll do that. Any case I like?'

'Er, yes, absolutely. Anything you like. Anything to keep you occupied.'

Hulda got the distinct impression that Magnús wanted her out of his office; he had more pressing matters to attend to.

'Great. I'll try to keep myself occupied then,' she said sarcastically, and getting to her feet, she walked out without a goodbye or a word of thanks.

V

Hulda stumbled back to her own office in a state of shock. She felt as if she'd been sacked, thrown out on her ear; as if all her years of service counted for nothing. It was an entirely new experience for her. She knew she was over-reacting, that she shouldn't take it like this, but couldn't seem to get rid of the sick feeling in the pit of her stomach.

She sat down at her desk and stared blankly at the computer, lacking the energy even to switch it on. Her office, which up to now had been like her second home, felt suddenly alien, as if the new owner had already taken possession. The old chair felt uncomfortable, the brown wooden desk looked tired and worn, the documents no longer meant anything to her. She couldn't bear the thought of spending another minute in there.

She needed a distraction, something to take her mind off what had happened. What better than to take Magnús at his word and dig around among the cold-case files? In reality, though, Hulda didn't need to think twice: there was one unsolved incident that cried out to be reopened.

The original investigation had been conducted by one of her colleagues – she had only followed its progress second hand – but that might prove an advantage, enabling her to approach the evidence with fresh eyes.

The case involved an unexplained death that would almost certainly remain a mystery unless new evidence came to light. Perhaps it would prove a blessing in disguise, a hidden opportunity. The dead woman had no one to speak up for her, but Hulda could take on the role of advocate, however briefly. Plenty could be achieved in two weeks. She didn't entertain any real hope of cracking the case, but it was worth trying. More than that, it would give her a purpose. She was grimly determined to turn up at the office every day until this 'young man' came to oust her. It crossed her mind to make an official complaint to HR about the way she was being treated and demand to see out the year, but there was time enough to think about that later. Right now, she wanted to direct her energies into something more positive.

Her first action was to call up the case file to refresh her memory of the details. The young woman's body had been found on a dark winter's morning in a rocky cove on Vatnsleysuströnd, a thinly populated stretch of coast on the Reykjanes peninsula, some thirty kilometres south of Reykjavík. Hulda had never been to that particular cove, had never had any particular reason to go there, though she was familiar with the area, having often driven past it on her way to the airport. It was a bleak, windswept corner of the country, the treeless lava-fields offering little shelter from the storms that regularly blew in from the Atlantic to the south-west.

In the year and more that had passed since then, the incident had faded from public memory. Not that it had attracted much media coverage at the time. After the usual reports that a body had been discovered, the follow-up had received little attention: the news spotlight had been directed elsewhere. Although Iceland was one of the safest countries in the world, with only around two murders a year – and sometimes not even one – accidental deaths were far more common and journalists felt there was little mileage in covering them.

It wasn't the media indifference that bothered Hulda; what concerned her was the suspicion that the CID colleague who had handled the case had been guilty of negligence. Alexander: she'd never had much faith in his abilities. In her opinion, he was neither diligent nor particularly bright, and he clung on to his position in CID only through a mixture of obstinacy and good connections. In a fairer world, she would have been promoted above him – she knew she was more intelligent, conscientious and experienced – but in spite of that she had remained stuck in the same rut. It was at times like this that she hadn't been able to resist a gnawing sense of bitterness. She would have given anything to have the authority to step in and wrest the case away from a detective who clearly wasn't up to the job.

Alexander's lack of enthusiasm for the inquiry had been glaringly obvious at team meetings when, in a bored voice, he had gone out of his way to present any evidence that pointed to accidental death. His report, as Hulda now discovered, was a sloppy piece of work. It included an unsatisfactorily brief summary of the post-mortem results, concluding with the usual proviso in the case of bodies washed up by the sea that it was impossible to establish if foul play was involved. Unsurprisingly, the investigation had turned up nothing useful and the inquiry had been moth-balled in favour of other 'more urgent' cases. Hulda couldn't help wondering how different the response might have been if the young woman had been Icelandic. What was the betting that the case would have been given to a more competent detective if the public had been clamouring for results?

The dead woman was twenty-seven years old, the age Hulda had been when she gave birth to her daughter. Only twenty-seven, in her prime: far too young to be the subject of a police investigation, of a cold case that no one seemed remotely interested in reopening, except Hulda.

According to the pathologist's report, she had drowned in salt water. Her head injuries were a possible indication that she had been subjected to violence beforehand, but she could, equally, have tripped, knocked herself out and fallen into the sea.

The victim's name was Elena; she was an asylum seeker from Russia and had only been in Iceland four months. Perhaps one reason Hulda found it so hard to let the matter lie was the speed at which everyone else had forgotten about Elena. She had come to a foreign country in search of refuge and found only a watery grave. And nobody cared. Hulda knew that, if she didn't seize this last chance to get to the bottom of the mystery, no one else would ever bother. Elena's story would pass into oblivion: she'd simply be the girl who came to Iceland and died.

VI

Hulda drove south out of Reykjavík, following what used to be her daily commute when they lived in their little house down by the sea on Álftanes. She hadn't been out there for years, not since the house was sold and she made the decision never to go back. The peninsula now appeared, low and green, across the bay to her right. Álftanes always used to feel semi-rural, its own little world, set apart from the urban sprawl of Reykjavík, but a whole new neighbourhood had sprung up there since her day.

As Álftanes dropped behind, taking her old life with it, she focused on her destination, the small town of Njardvík, which lay close to Keflavík airport on the Reykjanes peninsula. She was going to visit the asylum-seekers' hostel where, according to the case file, Elena had been living at the time of her death.

Hulda could have taken the rest of the day off and gone home. In spite of the rain, there was a hint of spring in the air. Now that May was here, you really began to notice how late it got dark, the light evenings holding out a promise of the midnight sun. It was a wonderful, life-affirming time of year, the darkness of the northern winter gradually receding, the evenings growing almost imperceptibly brighter every day until the middle of June, when the night was banished altogether. A vivid memory came back to her of those spectacular summer nights at their old place on Álftanes. Out in their back garden, where there was room to really breathe, you could watch the sun dipping below the sea while the sky flamed orange and red and the shore birds piped all night in the soft afterglow. In a cramped flat in a city apartment block, all the seasons seemed the same, the days merging in a monotonous blur and time slipping away with bewildering speed.

As if summer wasn't brief enough anyway. At its very height, in July, the darkness would begin its insidious return, creeping back into the lives of the islanders, first as no more than a hint of dusk, then by August, one of Hulda's least favourite months, the nights would have closed in again, a reminder that winter was at hand.

No, there could be no question of going home now, not after Magnús had dropped his bombshell. Cooped up between the four walls of her flat, she would go stir crazy, with nothing to distract her from the soul-destroying prospect of giving up work. Retirement was something Hulda had never mentally prepared herself for. It had been merely a date, a year, an age, all purely hypothetical. Until today, when it had suddenly become cold, hard fact.

Her thoughts snapped back to the present. She was

grateful for the stretches of dual carriageway where she could stick to the right-hand lane and allow the more impatient drivers to zip by. She drove an eighties Skoda, a relic of the times when most Icelanders drove around in affordable Eastern European cars – Soviet or Czech models, usually – from the countries with which Iceland traded fish. It was a bright-green, two-door model which had never had much acceleration and demanded an increasing amount of maintenance these days. Although practical, Hulda was no mechanic, but luckily she knew a man who lived for the chance to tinker with old cars and he kept the faithful Skoda on the road. For now.

It was a long time since Hulda had last driven south along this coast. She rarely had any need to go out to the Reykjanes peninsula. Even the international airport, the main draw in these parts, held little attraction for her. It wasn't that she didn't enjoy foreign travel – chance would be a fine thing – but her finances put the kibosh on any plans of that sort. Her police salary didn't stretch to over-seas holidays, not once she had covered her daily outgoings. In the old days, such luxuries had been com-fortably within reach. Her husband had run his own investment firm, with what she'd naively assumed to be a very respectable turnover, so it had come as a shock, after his sudden death, to learn that their financial security had been an illusion. Once the lawyers had unravelled his affairs, the inherited debts had turned out to exceed their assets. The upshot was that she'd had to sell their beauti-ful house and start again, almost from scratch, in middle age. She'd left the financial side of things entirely to her husband and never put aside any savings for herself, so it had proved far from easy to learn to live within her means on her new, tight budget. She had initially bought a small flat, which she had subsequently sold, and now she lived in a slightly larger flat in an apartment block. By incredible bad luck, she had upgraded to this place with an index-linked mortgage on the eve of the banking collapse and was now stuck with a massive debt and eye-wateringly high monthly repayments.

Hulda had always found the drive to the airport bleak and rather dispiriting. The dark lava-fields extended on either side, empty, windswept and flat, broken only by the conical form of Keilir and other low mountains to the south, and merging into the treacherous grey sea to the north. It was a dangerous area, full of hidden volcanic craters and clouds of steam, scarred by the violent forces at work beneath the earth's crust, here, where Iceland straddled the divide between two continental plates. The mountains were popular with hikers – Hulda had climbed quite a few of them herself – but otherwise this was a landscape better viewed from a distance than experienced on foot; anyone venturing into the lava-fields could so easily get injured and simply disappear.

But today the sun was shining out on the peninsula, although there was a blustery wind and, looking back across the bay, Hulda could see the rain clouds still hanging low over Reykjavík. Finally, a series of white apartment blocks with blue roofs rose from the featureless terrain to her right, signalling the outskirts of Njardvík, and she turned off into the town. It wasn't large but, as she didn't know her way around, it took her some time driving aimlessly through the streets before she finally located the hostel.

She hadn't called ahead to let them know she was coming; it hadn't even occurred to her in her haste to get out of the police station, away from the oppressive atmosphere that seemed to descend on the office the instant she got the bad news. She kept imagining that the corridors were full of people gossiping about her, that all her colleagues knew she'd been given the boot, that she was past it, surplus to requirements, ditched in favour of a younger model. Goddamnit.

The young woman at reception couldn't have been more than twenty-five. Hulda introduced herself as a police inspector without elaborating on the reason for her visit. The young woman didn't bat an eyelid.

'Oh, yes? What can I do for you? Do you need to speak to one of our residents?'

From what Hulda had been able to discover, the hostel was used exclusively as accommodation for asylum-seekers. It was an unwelcoming place. She could almost sense the desperation in the air, the silence and the tension. The walls were painted a stark white and there was nothing here to remind one of home or even of a hotel. This was a place where people waited in limbo to learn their fate.

'No, I'd just like a few words with whoever's in charge here.'

'Sure. That's me, Dóra.'

It took Hulda a moment to grasp that this young

woman was the hostel manager. 'Ah, right,' she said, embarrassed, ashamed of her own preconceptions. It hadn't even occurred to her that a mere slip of a girl like that could be in charge of running the place. 'Is there somewhere we could have a word in private?'

Dóra had short brown hair and a businesslike manner. Although her smile was friendly enough, her gaze was disconcertingly sharp. 'Of course, no problem,' she said. 'I've got an office round the back.'

She got up without another word and led the way briskly down the corridor, with Hulda following on her heels. The office was small and impersonal, with dark blinds over the windows and a single overhead bulb casting an unforgiving glare over the meagre contents. There were no books or papers, nothing but a laptop on the desk.

They sat down and Dóra waited, still without speaking, for Hulda to state her business. Casting around for the right words, Hulda began: 'The reason I'm here is . . . I'm investigating the death, a little over a year ago, of a woman who was one of your residents.'

'Death?'

'Yes. Her name was Elena. She was an asylum-seeker.'

'Oh, her. I'm with you. But . . .' Dóra frowned, puzzled. 'I thought the case was closed. He rang me – you know, the detective; I've forgotten his name . . .'

'Alexander,' Hulda supplied, picturing him as she said it: sleazy, overweight, with a blankness behind the eyes that never failed to set her teeth on edge.

'Yeah, Alexander, that was it. He rang to tell me he was closing the case because the investigation was

inconclusive and, personally, he thought it was an accident. Or suicide, maybe – Elena'd been waiting ages to
hear the result of her application.'

'Would you say she'd been waiting an abnormally long
time? It was my understanding that she'd been here four
months.'

'Oh no, not really – that's not unusual – but I guess the
waiting affects people differently. It can be stressful.'

'Did you agree with him?'

'Me?'

'Yes, you. Do you believe she drowned herself?'

'I'm no expert. I've no idea what I'm supposed to think.
It wasn't like I was the one investigating. Maybe
he – whatsisname . . .'

'Alexander.'

'Yeah, Alexander. Maybe he knew something I didn't.'
Dóra shrugged.

I very much doubt it, Hulda thought, suppressing
the temptation to say it aloud. 'But you must have
wondered.'

'Well, sure, but we're very busy here. People come and
go all the time: she happened to go like that. Anyway,
I don't have time to waste on wondering about that sort
of thing.'

'But surely you knew her?'

'Not really. No more than any of the others. Look, I'm
running a business here. This is how I make my living, so
I have to focus on the day-to-day management. It may be
a question of life or death for the residents, but I'm just
trying to run the place.'

'Is there someone else here who might have known her better?'

Dóra appeared to think about this. 'I doubt it. Not any more. Like I said, people come and go all the time.'

'So, let me get this straight: you're saying that none of your current residents would have been here when Elena was alive?'

'Oh, well, there's always a possibility . . .'

'Would you be able to check?'

'I suppose so.'

Dóra turned to the laptop and started clicking away. Finally, she looked up. 'Two Iraqi guys – they're still here. You can meet them in a minute. And a Syrian woman.'

'Can I meet her, too?'

'I doubt it.'

'Why's that?'

'She's out and about somewhere. Her lawyer came by earlier and I think they went into Reykjavík. There's been some progress on her case, which is just as well, seeing as all she does is shut herself away in her room and wait. She hardly even comes down for meals. That's all I know – the lawyers don't tell me a thing, of course – but I guessed from looking at them that something was up. Let's hope it's good news, though you can never be sure.'

'Tell me about Elena. How did she behave? What was her situation?'

'Haven't a clue.'

'Did she have a lawyer working on her case?'

'Yes, I assume so – though I can't remember who it was, if I ever knew.'

'Well, do you have any idea who it might have been?'

'It tends to be the same people,' Dóra said, and reeled off three names, which Hulda duly noted down.

'Would it be possible to see her room?'

'Why are the police looking into this again?' Dóra asked.

'Look, could you just show me her room?' Hulda snapped, her patience running out.

'All right, all right,' Dóra said huffily. 'It wouldn't hurt to show some manners, you know. It's no joke getting mixed up in this sort of thing.'

'Are you mixed up in it?'

'Oh, you know what I mean. Her room's upstairs, but there's someone else using it now. We can't just barge in on him.'

'Could you at least check if he's in?'

Dóra flounced out of the office, along the corridor and up the stairs, with Hulda hastily following. After passing several doors, Dóra came to a halt by one and knocked. A young man answered and Dóra explained in English that the police wanted to see his room. Clearly alarmed, the man asked haltingly: 'They want send me home?' He repeated the question several times before Dóra could reassure him that the police visit had nothing to do with him. Almost tearful with relief, he nodded reluctantly, though Hulda knew he wasn't legally obliged to let them in. Then again, it was unlikely the poor man would have dared to insist on his rights to the representative of a foreign police force. She felt a little ashamed of herself for putting him through this. Still, the ends justified the means. She didn't have much time.

'Did she speak English?' Hulda asked Dóra, once they were inside the room. Its current occupant remained standing awkwardly outside in the corridor.

'Sorry?' Dóra glanced round.

'The Russian girl. Elena.'

'Very little. She could maybe understand a bit, but she couldn't carry on a conversation in English, only in Russian.'

'Was that why you didn't get to know her?'

Dóra shook her head, looking amused. 'Oh no, I don't get to know any of them, regardless of what language they speak.'

'There's not a lot of room in here.'

'I'm not running a luxury hotel,' Dóra said.

'Did she have the room to herself?'

'Yes. And she wasn't much trouble, as far as I can remember.'

'Not much trouble?'

'Yes. Didn't make a fuss – you know what I mean. Not all of them can handle the waiting. It can be tough.'

The narrow, cell-like room contained a bed, a tiny desk and a wardrobe of sorts. There were few personal items, apart from a pair of tracksuit bottoms lying on the bed and a half-eaten toasted sandwich on the desk.

'No TV?' Hulda remarked.

'Like I said, this isn't a luxury hotel. There's a TV down in the lounge.'

'Any chance she might have left some of her belongings behind?'

'Can't remember, I'm afraid. If people vanish and don't show up again, I usually chuck their things out.'

'Or if they die.'

'Yes.'

There was little to be learned from the room, at first glance, anyway. Hulda took another quick look around her, if only to try to put herself in the shoes of the dead girl; get an impression of what her life must have been like during those last few months, cast adrift in a strange country at an unfriendly hostel where no one spoke her language. Trapped within the four walls of a small room, just as Hulda sometimes felt like a prisoner in her own flat, all alone, no family, no one to care for her. That was the worst part – having no one who cared.

Just for a second, Hulda closed her eyes and tried to breathe in the atmosphere, but all she could smell was mushroom soup wafting through the building from the kitchen.

VII

Before she left, Hulda had a brief word with the two men from Iraq. The one who did the talking spoke quite good English. They had been living in Iceland for over a year and were obviously grateful for the chance to speak to a police officer, apparently regarding her as a representative of the authorities. Before she could ask the questions she wanted, Hulda was forced to listen to a stream of complaints about the way their cases were being handled and the treatment they'd had to put up with. When she was finally able to get a word in edgeways, she established that they did remember Elena, though mainly because of her sudden death. It turned out they had never actually spoken to her, as they didn't know a word of Russian, so there was very little to be gained from the conversation.

On her way out through reception, Hulda thanked Dóra and asked her to get in touch when the Syrian woman turned up, in the faint hope that she might know something. 'I'll do that,' Dóra promised, but Hulda wasn't under any illusion that she would make it a priority.

Three quarters of an hour later, Hulda was back in Reykjavík. She parked outside the police station but had no real intention of going inside. Instead, she set about trying to find out which lawyer had been handling Elena's case. It took no more than a couple of phone calls to establish that the man she wanted was a middle-aged solicitor who had worked for the police for several years before leaving to set up his own firm. He remembered Hulda immediately.

'I doubt there's much I can tell you,' he said in a friendly voice, 'but you're welcome to drop by. You know where we are?'

'I'll find you. Can I come over now?'

'Please do,' he said.

The solicitor's office turned out to be a modest affair in the city centre that didn't even run to a reception-ist. Albert Albertsson, who had come out to greet Hulda in person, seemed to read her mind: 'We run a tight little outfit here,' he explained. 'Don't waste any money on frills. We all turn our hand to whatever needs doing. Anyway, it's nice to see you again.'

Albert had always had an easy manner and spoke in the warm, well-modulated tones of a congenial late-night radio host chatting to listeners against a background of soothing music. By no stretch of the imagination could you call him good-looking, but he had the kind of face that inspired trust.

The office Albert showed her into couldn't have presented a greater contrast to Dóra's bare, soulless little workspace at the hostel. The walls were hung with paintings, there were photographs lined up on the shelf beside the desk and towering stacks of papers on every available surface. Hulda found it slightly overwhelming. It felt a bit over the top, like an attempt to cover up the fact that maybe Albert didn't actually have that much to do. All the photographs and paintings would have been better suited to a home than a workplace. Unless this was all the home he really had?

'Have you taken over the case?' he asked, once they were seated.

Hulda barely hesitated: 'Yes, for now.'

'Any developments?'

'Nothing I can comment on at present,' she replied. 'Did Alexander speak to you in the course of the original inquiry?'

'Yes, he did. We had a meeting, but I don't think I was able to help him much.'

'Did you handle Elena's asylum application from the beginning?'

'I did. I take on a lot of these human-rights jobs. Alongside my other work, of course.'

'Could you fill me in on the background to her case?'

'Well, she was claiming asylum in Iceland on the grounds that she'd suffered persecution at home in Russia.'

'But her application was unsuccessful?'

'What? No, on the contrary, we were making good progress.'

'How good?'

'They were about to allow her claim.'

Hulda was completely wrong-footed. 'Hang on a minute: you're saying they were going to grant her asylum?'

'Yes, it was in the pipeline.'

'Was she aware of this?'

'Yes, of course. She heard the day before she died.'

'Did you tell Alexander?'

'Naturally, though I don't really see how it's relevant.'

Alexander had 'forgotten' to mention the fact in his report.

'Well, it reduces the likelihood that she'd have taken her own life,' Hulda pointed out.

'Not necessarily,' Albert argued. 'The whole process puts the applicants under a huge amount of strain.'

'How did she strike you – in general, I mean? Was she the cheerful type? Or inclined to be depressive?'

'Hard to say.' Albert leaned forward over his desk. 'Hard to say,' he repeated, 'since she spoke very little English and I don't know any Russian.'

'You used an interpreter, then?'

'Yes, when required. The process generated quite a bit of paperwork.'

'Maybe I should talk to the interpreter,' Hulda muttered, more to herself than to Albert.

'If you think it'll help. His name's Bjartur. He lives in the west of town, works from home. But it's all in the files. You can borrow them, if you'd like.'

'Thanks, that would be great.'

'She was musical,' Albert added suddenly, as an afterthought.

'Musical?'

'Yes, I gather she loved music. My partner keeps a guitar in the office and Elena once picked it up and strummed a couple of tunes for us.'

'What else did you know about her?' Hulda asked.

'What else . . . ? Nothing much,' Albert replied. 'We never really learn much about the asylum-seekers we represent, and I try not to get too personal. They usually get sent back, you know.' He was silent for a moment, then added: 'It was all very sad. The poor girl. But then, suicide always is.'

'Suicide?'

'Yes. Wasn't that what Alexander's investigation concluded?'

'Yes, quite. Alexander's investigation.'

VIII

'I thought the case was closed.' The interpreter, Bjartur, settled himself in an office chair so old and rickety it must have dated back to the eighties. 'But, if not, I'd be glad to offer any help I can.'

'Thanks. Did Alexander talk to you at the time? Were you able to provide him with any information?'

'Alexander?' Bjartur's face was blank under his handsome blond mane. He was well named. Bjartur meant 'bright'. They were sitting in a converted garage, attached to a small detached house in an affluent suburb in the west of town. Surrounded by sea on three sides, the location was pleasant, if windy. When Hulda arrived, she'd rung the bell by the front door and an elderly lady had directed her round to the garage 'where Bjartur has his office'. There was no chair for visitors, so Hulda made do with perching on the edge of an old bed that was buried under books, many of them in Russian, or so she deduced from the lettering on the spines. Although she had called ahead to warn him she was coming, Bjartur seemed to have made no effort to tidy up. The floor was littered with piles of papers, walking boots and pizza boxes, and there was a heap of dirty clothes in one corner.

'Alexander's a colleague of mine from CID,' she explained, a bad taste in her mouth. 'He was in charge of the investigation.'

'Oh, well, I never met him. You're the first person who's ever spoken to me about this.'

Hulda felt the bitter resentment flaring up inside her again. If she'd been promoted above Alexander, as she'd deserved, she'd have given him his marching orders long ago.

'What's up?' asked Bjartur, breaking into her thoughts. 'Has something new come to light?'

Hulda resorted to the same answer she had given the lawyer earlier: 'Nothing I can comment on at present.' The truth was that she had nothing to go on apart from a gut feeling, but there was no need to admit the fact. Besides, the conviction had been steadily growing inside her all day that her decision to reopen the inquiry had been the right one: whatever the cause of Elena's death, it was obvious that the original investigation had been disgracefully slack. 'Did you meet her often?'

'Not that often, no. I take on these jobs when they come up. They don't involve a lot of work and the pay's pretty good. It's hard to live off translation alone.'

'But you manage?'

'Just about. I do quite a bit of interpreting for Russians, some of it for people in the same situation as . . . um . . .'

'Elena,' prompted Hulda. Not even Bjartur could remember her name. It was extraordinary how quickly the girl's presence in Iceland was fading from people's memories: no one gave a damn about her, it seemed.

'Elena – of course. Yes, now and then I interpret for people in her situation, but I mainly work as a tour guide for Russians, showing them the sights. Some of them are rolling in it, so the pay's not bad. Apart from that, I translate the odd short story or book, even do a bit of writing myself –'

'What was your impression of her?' Hulda interrupted. 'Did she seem suicidal at all?'

'Now you're asking,' Bjartur said, thwarted in his desire to talk about himself. 'Hard to say. Maybe. As you'd expect, she wasn't exactly happy here. But wasn't it . . . I mean, surely it must have been suicide?'

'Probably not, actually,' said Hulda, with unwarranted confidence. She had a hunch that the interpreter knew more than he was letting on. The trick was to avoid putting too much pressure on him: all she had to do was be patient and allow him to open up in his own time. 'Did you study in Russia?' she asked.

He seemed a little thrown by this abrupt change of subject. 'What? Oh, yes. At Moscow State University. I fell in love with the city and the language. Ever been there yourself?'

Hulda shook her head.

'It's an amazing place. You should visit sometime.'

'Right,' said Hulda, knowing she never would.

'Amazing, but challenging,' Bjartur went on. 'A

challenging place to be a tourist. Everything's so alien: the language, the Cyrillic script.'

'But your Russian's fluent, isn't it?'

'Oh, sure,' he said airily, 'but then I got the hang of it years ago.'

'So you had no problem communicating with Elena?'

'Problem? No, of course not.'

'So what did you two talk about?'

'Not much, really,' he admitted. 'Mostly, I just interpreted for her at meetings with her lawyer.'

'He mentioned that she was keen on music,' Hulda said, in an effort to keep the conversation moving forward.

'Oh, yes, that's right. As a matter of fact, she did talk to me about that. She writes . . . used to write music. She had no chance of doing it professionally in Russia, but that was the dream: to work as a composer here. She played a tune for us once at the lawyer's office. She was quite good – well, not bad, you know. But it was totally unrealistic. No one can make a living as a composer in Iceland.'

'Any more than they can as a translator?'

Bjartur smiled but didn't rise to this. Instead, after a brief pause, he said: 'Actually, there *was* something else . . .'

'Something else?' Hulda asked encouragingly. She could tell from his expression that he was in two minds about whether to go on.

'You'd better keep it to yourself, though.'

'Keep what to myself?'

'Look, I don't want to get dragged into anything . . . I can't . . .'

'What happened?' Hulda asked, employing her friendliest voice.

'It was just something she said . . . By the way, this is strictly off the record.'

Hulda forced herself to smile politely, resisting the urge to point out the difference between a police officer and a journalist. Although she had no intention of making any promises, she maintained a diplomatic silence, not wishing to frighten him off.

Her tactic worked. After a moment's hesitation, Bjartur continued: 'I think she might have been on the game.'

'On the game? Working as a prostitute, you mean?' Hulda asked. 'What reason do you have for thinking that?'

'She told me.'

'This didn't come out in any of the reports,' Hulda said angrily, though her anger was directed more at the absent figure of Alexander than at Bjartur.

'No, it wouldn't have. She told me the first time we met but insisted she didn't want anyone else to know. I got the feeling she was scared.'

'Of what?'

'Of who, you mean.'

'An Icelander?'

'Not sure.' He wavered, seeming to think it over. 'To be honest, I got the impression from what she said that she'd been brought over to Iceland solely for that purpose.'

'Are you serious? You mean her application for asylum was just a cover?'

'It's possible. She was a bit vague about the whole thing, but it was very obvious that she didn't want the news to get out.'

'So her lawyer didn't know?'

'I don't think so, no. I certainly didn't tell him anything. I kept her secret.' After a beat, he added, a little ashamed: 'Until now, of course.'

'Why on earth didn't you tell anyone?' Hulda demanded, sounding harsher than she'd intended.

There was another brief pause, then Bjartur replied, rather lamely: 'Nobody asked.'

IX

The young mother walked home as usual, but this evening she was unusually tired. It had been a long day at Hótel Borg, the weather had been dark and dreary, the wind and rain dragging her down. Her job description at the landmark hotel in the town centre was rather vague; sometimes she was asked to clean the guestrooms and other times she helped out in the restaurant and bar, often well into the night. She took any shift she was offered, as long as it didn't interfere with her visits to her daughter.

It had been a day of celebration, 1 December, Sovereignty Day, commemorating Iceland's achievement of partial independence from Denmark thirty years earlier, in 1918. Students had gathered at the hotel during the evening for a party, and there had been lots of singing and speeches, and the well-known poet Tómas Gudmundsson had performed some of his works.

Christmas was fast approaching and she wanted to buy a present for her daughter, although she wasn't sure what to get her. It had to be something special, that was all she knew. And she had to have some money to buy the gift. There was this film she really wanted to see at the Gamla Bíó, *Boom Town*, starring Clark Gable, but she would probably have to give it a miss, as she was saving every penny for her daughter.

How she had envied those young students tonight. How she had longed to be one of them. She knew she had the potential to make something of herself, but that it would never be fulfilled. Iceland was supposed to be a classless society, everyone was supposed to be equal, with no upper, middle or lower class. Everyone was supposed to have an equal chance of succeeding. But she knew this was a myth; she would never rise above her current status, working in low-paid jobs, with no security. A single mother from a poor background. She didn't stand a chance.

But she was determined that things would be different for her daughter.

X

Bjartur's revelation had put Hulda's investigation – if you could call it an investigation – in a whole new light. This was dynamite. Not only had Alexander's inquiry been exposed as perfunctory in the extreme, but the Russian girl's death had acquired an entirely new angle. The question was at what point Hulda should inform her boss of this fresh twist. At the moment, Magnús didn't even know which cold case she had chosen to reopen. No doubt he was busy congratulating himself on the neat way in which he had edged her out and, if he thought about her at all, would assume she was sitting at her desk, poring over old police files to while away the time as the clock ticked inexorably towards her retirement.

In fact, she hadn't been near CID since this morning's fateful meeting. To her surprise, the day had passed far more quickly than she had feared: all that rushing around had left her with no time at all to wallow in self-pity. She had the rest of the evening for that. But, no – she was planning to get an early night, have a good long sleep to clear her head, and put off any decision about what to do next until the morning. She could make up her mind then whether she had the energy – and the courage – to completely immerse herself in the Russian girl's case or whether she should simply throw in the towel and start getting used to life as a pensioner. Admit to herself that her career in the police was over. Stop trying to resist the inevitable. Stop chasing phantoms that may never have existed.

Whatever her eventual decision, there was one loose end she still needed to tie up. Settling herself in her mother's comfy old chair, phone in hand, she deliberated for a while, putting off dialling the number of the wretched nurse she had questioned the day before; the woman who had run down that evil bastard of a paedophile and shaken like a leaf from nerves and guilt throughout the interview. She must be going through a private hell right now, worried sick about being parted from her son and having to spend years behind bars. After all, she had confessed. But, so far, Hulda had not only failed to write up a formal report of their conversation, she had actually lied to her boss and said that the case was nowhere near being solved. The question she had to debate with her conscience, before ringing the poor woman, was whether to stick to the lie and do her damnedest to spare the mother and son any further injustice, or to write the truth in her report, in the knowledge that the woman would almost inevitably be sent down for her crime.

The answer was never really in doubt: there was only one course of action open to Hulda.

The woman had a mobile and a home phone number registered to her name. She didn't answer the mobile and her landline rang for ages before she finally picked up. Hulda introduced herself: 'This is Hulda Hermanns-dóttir, from CID. We spoke yesterday.'

'Oh . . . yes . . . of course,' said the woman in a strangled voice. She drew a deep, shuddering breath.

'I've been reviewing the incident,' Hulda lied, resorting to deliberately formal police speak, 'and I've come to the conclusion that we don't have sufficient evidence to convict.'

'What . . . what do you mean?' the woman stammered. She sounded as if she was crying.

'I'm not planning to take things any further, not as far as you're concerned.'

There was a stunned silence at the other end, then the woman croaked: 'But what about . . . what about the thing I told you?'

'It wouldn't serve any purpose to pursue it further, to drag you through the courts.'

Again, there was a silence. Then: 'You . . . you mean you're not going to . . . arrest me? I . . . I've hardly stopped shaking since . . . since we spoke. I thought I was going to –'

'Quite. No, I'm not going to arrest you. And seeing as I'm about to retire, with any luck, this should be the last you hear of the matter.' *Retire.* It was the first time she'd said it out loud and the word echoed oddly in her ears. She was struck yet again by how ridiculously unprepared she was for this milestone, foreseeable though it had been.

'What about the other . . . what about your colleagues in the police?'

'Don't worry, I won't mention your confession in my report. Of course, I can't predict what'll happen to the case after I leave, but as far as I'm concerned, you didn't admit to anything when I interviewed you. Have I got that right?'

'What? Oh, yes, of course. Thank you . . .'

Something compelled Hulda to add: 'But don't get me wrong: this doesn't absolve you from guilt. Maybe I can understand why you did what you did, but the fact is that you're going to have to live with it. Still, in my opinion, locking you up and depriving your son of his mother would only make matters worse.'

'Thank you,' the woman repeated in heartfelt tones, her sobbing now clearly audible down the line. 'Thank you,' she managed to gasp again before Hulda rang off.

When busy or under pressure, Hulda often forgot to eat, but she made sure she had something now. Her supper was the same as last night's: cheese on toast. Since Jón died, she had given up cooking altogether. At first, she had tried to make the effort, but as the years went by and she got used to living alone, she'd made do with a hot meal in the work canteen at midday and survived mainly on a diet of fast food or sandwiches in the evenings.

She was in the middle of her simple snack, listening to the radio news, when the phone rang. Seeing who it was, she felt an impulse to ignore it, but habit and a sense of duty made her pick up. Characteristically, he launched straight in without even bothering to give his name, but then Alexander had never had any manners: 'What the hell are you playing at?' he stormed. She pictured him at the other end: features twisted in a scowl, the double chin, the drooping eyelids under heavy brows.

She wasn't going to let him fluster her. 'What are you talking about?' she asked in as normal a voice as she could manage.

'Come off it, Hulda. You know as well as I do. For fuck's sake. That Russian girl who drowned herself.'

'Can't you even remember her name?'

The question apparently caught him off-guard. He was speechless for a moment, which was unlike him. But he soon recovered. 'What's that got to do with anything? What I want to –'

'Her name was Elena,' Hulda interrupted.

'I don't give a shit!' His voice rose. No doubt his face had flushed dark red. 'Why are you sticking your nose into this, Hulda? I thought you'd left.'

So the news had spread.

'You must have been misinformed,' she said levelly.

'Oh? From what I heard . . .' He thought better of it. 'Whatever. Why are you muscling in on my case?'

'Because Magnús asked me to,' Hulda said. This was stretching the truth, but never mind.

'You're deliberately trying to undermine me, that's what this is. I've already dealt with that case.'

'Not in a way that does you any credit,' Hulda said coolly.

'There was nothing dodgy about it,' Alexander blustered, almost shouting now. 'The poor cow was about to be deported so she threw herself in the sea. End of story.'

'On the contrary, her request for asylum was about to be granted, and she knew it.'

There was a sudden silence at the other end. After a moment, Alexander spluttered: 'What? What are you talking about?'

'The case is far from closed, that's all there is to it. And you're interrupting my supper, so if there's nothing else . . .'

'Interrupting your supper? Yeah, right – a lonely sandwich in front of the TV,' he said nastily. Having delivered this parting shot, he hung up.

That was below the belt. The truth was that she was always alone; the only single woman among a group of men, most of whom were married, if not to their first, then to their second wives, and surrounded by big extended families. It wasn't the first time she'd been the butt of this kind of remark. It went with the territory, along with the tasteless jokes, the outright bullying. She could be prickly in her dealings with other people, she knew, but then she'd had to develop a thick skin to survive, and in return it seemed this gave the lads a licence to take pot shots at her.

Of course, she should have been able to shrug off Alexander's spiteful dig but, instead, to prove him wrong, she decided to call Pétur from the walking club. She still thought of him as a friend rather than a boyfriend – their relationship felt too platonic for that. Whenever they were together she found herself wishing she was twenty, thirty years younger; then it wouldn't have been as hard to make that next move, progress from the polite pecks on the cheek to something more intimate. Then again, there were times on the phone to him when she felt as shy as a girl again; a sign, she thought, that their relationship was on the right track, that maybe she did want more.

As usual, he was quick to answer. Typically brisk and on the ball.

'I wondered,' she said diffidently, 'that is, I wondered if you'd like to pop over for coffee this evening.' The moment the words had slipped out, she realized they could be misconstrued. Inviting a man round for coffee out of the blue like that . . . She wanted to add that she wasn't asking him to spend the night, but she bit her lip and merely hoped he wouldn't read more into her offer than she'd intended.

'I'd love to,' he answered, without a moment's hesitation. He was always decisive, never one to get bogged down in details or make a mountain out of a molehill; qualities Hulda appreciated. Nevertheless, this was quite a big step for them, as she'd never invited him round to her place before. Was it that she was ashamed of her flat? she wondered. In comparison to their old house on Álftanes with its big windows and large garden – yes, maybe. But mainly it was due to the invisible defences she had raised around herself, defences she'd been reluctant to lower for him until now, when, in desperate need of company, she had decided to take the risk.

'Shall I come round now?' he asked.

'Yes, sure, that would be great. If you can.' She was ridiculously insecure when talking to him; it was so unlike her. Usually, she had every aspect of her life well under control.

'Of course. Where do you live?'

She reeled off her address, finishing: 'Fourth floor, my name's on the bell.'

'I'll be straight over,' he said, and rang off without saying goodbye.

'About time you invited me round,' was Pétur's first comment when she opened the door. At getting on for seventy, he was a few years older than Hulda but wore his age well, looking neither much younger nor much older than he really was, though his grey beard did give him a slightly grandfatherly air. Hulda couldn't stop herself from wondering, just for an instant, what Jón would have looked like at seventy.

Almost before she knew what was happening, Pétur was in the sitting room, making himself comfortable in her favourite chair. Hulda felt a twinge of irritation: her mother's armchair was her spot, but of course she didn't say this aloud. After all, she was pleased to have him there, happy that someone wanted to spend the evening with her. She had got used to the loneliness, as far as this was possible, but there was no real substitute for the company of another human being. She had sometimes tried going out by herself, to restaurants for lunch or dinner, but it had made her feel self-conscious and embarrassed, so now she tended to eat in the office canteen or alone at home.

She asked if he'd like a coffee.

'Thanks, no milk.'

Pétur was a doctor. He'd taken early retirement at sixty,

when his wife fell ill, and had told Hulda, without going into any details, that they'd managed some good years together before the end. This information was enough for her to be going on with; she had no wish to make him relive his grief and hoped he would be similarly understanding about not requiring her to reopen old wounds. All she had told him was that Jón had died suddenly at fifty-two. 'Long before his time,' she had added, stating the obvious.

Beneath Pétur's comfortable manner there was a hint of steel, a combination which Hulda guessed would have made him a good doctor. He'd certainly done well for himself. She had visited his large house in the desirable neighbourhood of Fossvogur. It was spacious, with high ceilings and a living room graced with handsome furniture, oil paintings on the walls, a wide selection of books on the shelves and even a grand piano taking pride of place in the middle. Ever since seeing it, she had entertained fantasies about living there, spending her days ensconced in a lovely living room in a cultured home. She could ditch her dreary high-rise apartment, use the cash to pay off her debts and enjoy a comfortable retirement in a large house in a nice neighbourhood. But, of course, that wasn't the main reason; the truth was she felt good in Pétur's company, and she was gradually coming to the realization that she might be ready to move on, to commit again after all these years of loneliness.

'I've had quite a day,' she said, before stepping into the kitchen to fetch the coffee she'd made in advance.

When she came back into the cramped sitting room and handed Pétur a cup, he smiled his thanks and waited for her to continue with what she had been saying, radiating patience and sympathy. He'd been a surgeon, but she thought he'd have made an excellent psychiatrist: he was a man who knew how to listen.

'I'm stopping work,' she said, when the silence grew uncomfortable.

'That was on the cards, wasn't it?' he said. 'It's not as bad as it sounds, you know. You'll have more time for your hobbies, more time to enjoy life.'

He certainly knew how to do that, she reflected, allowing a moment of envy to sour her thoughts. As a doctor with a successful career behind him, he didn't have to face any financial worries in his old age.

'Yes, it was on the cards,' she agreed in a low voice, 'but not quite yet.' Best to be honest with him, not try to embellish the facts. 'To tell the truth, I've been given my marching orders. I've only got two weeks left. They've hired some boy in my place.'

'Bloody hell. And you took that lying down? It doesn't sound like you.'

'Well,' she said, mentally cursing herself for not having put up more of a fight when Magnús broke the news, 'at least I managed to wangle one final case out of my boss, to finish on.'

'Now you're talking. Anything interesting?'

'A murder . . . I think.'

'Are you serious? Two weeks to solve a murder? You're not worried you won't succeed and that it'll prey on your mind after you retire?'

She hadn't thought of that, but Pétur had a point.

'Too late to back out now,' she said, without much conviction. 'Anyway, it's not a hundred per cent certain that it was murder.'

'What's the case about?' he asked, managing to sound genuinely interested.

'A young woman found dead in a cove on Vatnsleysuströnd.'

'Recently?'

'More than a year ago.'

Pétur frowned. 'I don't remember that.'

'It didn't attract much media coverage at the time. She was an asylum-seeker.'

'An asylum-seeker . . . No, I definitely didn't hear about that.'

Not many people did, Hulda thought.

'How did she die?' he asked.

'She drowned, but there were injuries on her body. The detective who handled the case – not one of our best men, I might add – dismissed it as suicide. I'm not so sure.'

Feeling pleased with the progress she'd made that day, she gave him a brief account of her discoveries but, to her disappointment, Pétur looked sceptical.

'Are you sure,' he asked hesitantly, 'are you sure you're not building this up to be bigger than it really is?'

Hulda was a little taken aback by his frankness, but another part of her appreciated it.

'No, I'm not at all sure,' she admitted. 'But I'm determined to follow it up.'

'Fair enough,' he said.

*

It was getting late. They had swapped their coffee for red wine a couple of hours ago. Pétur had stayed longer than anticipated but, far from complaining, Hulda welcomed the company. The rain clouds had finally departed, making way for the sun, and the sky was deceptively light outside, belying the lateness of the hour.

The wine hadn't been Hulda's idea. After finishing his coffee, Pétur had asked if she happened to have a drop of brandy, and she apologized but said she did have a couple of bottles of wine knocking about somewhere.

'I like the sound of that. Good for the old ticker,' he'd said, and who was she to question the word of a medical man?

'It strikes me as a bit unusual,' Pétur remarked warily, feeling his way, 'that you don't have any family photos on display.'

The observation took Hulda by surprise, but she tried to sound casual: 'I've never been one for that kind of thing. I don't know why.'

'I suppose I understand. I probably have too many photos of my wife around the place. Maybe that's why it's taken me so long to get over her. I'm stuck in the past, quite literally.' He heaved a sigh. They were on to their second bottle now. 'What about your parents? Your brothers and sisters? No pictures of them either?'

'I don't have any brothers or sisters,' Hulda said. She didn't immediately go on, but Pétur waited patiently, sipping his wine. 'My mother and I were never particularly close,' she said eventually, as if justifying the absence of photographs, though there was no reason why she should have to make excuses.

'How long ago did she die?'

'Fifteen years ago. She wasn't that old, only seventy,' Hulda said, conscious of how scarily soon she would be that age herself: in just over five years. And the last five years had gone by in a flash.

'She can't have been very old when she had you,' Pétur remarked, after doing some quick mental arithmetic.

'Twenty . . . though I don't think that would have counted as particularly young in those days.'

'And your father?'

'Never met him.'

'Really? Did he die before you were born?'

'No. I just never knew him – he was a foreigner.' Her thoughts wandered back. 'Actually, once, years ago, I did go abroad to try and trace him, but that's another story . . .'

She smiled politely at Pétur. Though she tolerated these personal questions, she wasn't keen on them. No doubt he expected her to respond in kind, by asking about his family and past life, to bring them closer. But that wasn't going to happen. Not yet. She felt she knew enough about him to be going on with: he'd lost his wife and lived alone (in a house that was far too big for him), and, more importantly, he came across as a decent, kind man; honest and reliable. That would do for Hulda.

'Yes,' he said, breaking the silence, sounding a little tipsy now. 'We're two lonely souls, all right. Some people take the decision early in life . . . to be alone, I mean. But in our case, I think it was fate.' He paused. 'My wife and I made a conscious decision to put off having children – until it was too late for us to change our minds. Towards the end, we often discussed whether it had been a mistake.' After a moment, he added: 'I don't believe in having regrets: life is what it is, it plays out one way or another. But having said that, I really wish I weren't so alone at this point in mine.'

Hulda hadn't been expecting this level of candour. She didn't know what to say, and after a brief silence Pétur went on: 'I don't know how you two ended up childless, and I don't mean to pry, but that sort of thing, decisions like that, they have a profound impact on our lives. They matter, really matter. Don't you agree?'

Hulda nodded, glancing discreetly at the clock, then at the bottle, and Pétur got the hint: it was time to say goodnight.

XI

No matter how busy she was, she always turned up punctually to visit her daughter. Twice a week without fail, never missing a day. However heavy the snow or fierce the storm. Not even illness could deter her, since the glass dividing them ensured that she couldn't infect her baby. Twice now these visits had landed her in trouble with unsympathetic employers, and on the second occasion she had handed in her notice. Her daughter came first.

Physically at least, the little girl appeared to be thriving. Her second birthday was rapidly approaching and she was healthy and tall for her age, but there was a far away look in her eyes that made her mother anxious.

Perhaps, deep down, she knew that too long had passed: that her visits weren't achieving anything; that the invisible thread connecting mother and daughter had snapped at some point during these two years of separation. Maybe it had happened at the very beginning, on the day when, against her will, she had relinquished her daughter into the hands of strangers. Her parents, ashamed of their daughter for having a child out of wedlock and wishing to hush up the affair, had considered it for the best. They had presented her with a stark choice: either give the child up for adoption – something she would never dream of doing – or place her in an institution for infants 'to start off with'.

She had been living with her parents when her baby was born and couldn't afford to move into a place of her own, so for her the choice was simple: since giving up her baby for good was out of the question, the second option had seemed the lesser of two evils.

After finishing her compulsory schooling, she hadn't taken any further qualifications, and felt it was too late to make up for that now. In any case, her parents had never encouraged her to get an education, placing all their expectations instead on the shoulders of her younger brother, who was now at Reykjavík College.

But things were about to change. She had been working for two years, putting money aside, and, although she was still living with her parents, it wouldn't be long before she could afford to move out into her own flat. And then she could realize her long-desired dream of reclaiming her daughter from the institution.

Her relationship with her parents had become increasingly strained. At first, too numb to stand up to them when she fell unexpectedly pregnant, she had allowed them to push her around. Now, she was afraid she would never be able to forgive them for parting her from her child. Looking back, she couldn't understand how she had ever agreed to such a thing.

She only hoped her little girl would find it in her heart to forgive her.

XII

After saying goodbye to Pétur with a chaste kiss on the cheek, Hulda went back into the sitting room and reclaimed the old armchair. She was too restless to go to bed straight away, couldn't face being alone in the dark with only her thoughts for company. There were too many of them circling, waiting to pounce, each more upsetting than the last.

The Russian girl was still uppermost in her mind, though she had pushed the thought of her away while drinking wine with Pétur. The wine – good point: there was still a splash left. No call to waste it. Reaching for the bottle, Hulda tipped the dregs into her glass. The Russian girl . . . But thinking about Elena inevitably brought Hulda round full circle to the circumstances in which the young woman's death had ended up on her desk: she had, to all intents and purposes, been given her notice today; told to clear out her office; swept out of the way like a piece of old rubbish.

In an effort to distract herself, she started to think

about Pétur, but that was problematic, too, because she didn't want to risk investing too much hope in the future of their relationship. His visit had gone well, but now they needed to take the next step. She didn't want to lose him, and she was scared that if she took things too slowly she might end up closing the door completely. And, realistically, how many more opportunities would she get?

Caught in this dilemma, she sat gazing abstractedly into her glass, taking occasional sips of wine, until, creeping out of the dark recesses of her mind, came the figures she didn't want to think about, the figures she never *stopped* thinking about: Jón and her daughter.

At long last, she felt her eyelids drooping and knew she was tired enough to go to bed, safe in the knowledge that she would be able to get off to sleep without being tortured unnecessarily by her inner demons.

For once, she switched off the alarm clock on her bedside table, the clock that had for so many years woken her punctually at 6 a.m. every weekday, almost without exception. Well, this time the clock could have a rest, and so could Hulda. Without giving it much thought, she also switched her phone to silent, something she rarely did, as her job was all important to her and she liked to be available day and night. You couldn't always, or maybe ever, conduct complex police investigations within normal office hours.

Closing her eyes, she let herself float away into the world of dreams.

Day Two

I

Hulda was stunned to discover that it was nearly eleven o'clock. She couldn't remember the last time she had slept so late. The light was on in her bedroom, as usual. She didn't like sleeping in the dark.

Disbelieving, she checked her alarm clock again, but there was no doubt. Her accumulated tiredness must have caught up with her. She lay there for a while, luxuriating in the fact that she wasn't in a hurry for once, and as she did so, snatches of her dreams came back to her. Elena had turned up: Hulda could remember travelling back to Njardvík, to that comfortless little cell at the hostel. She couldn't recapture all the details, only the sense that the dream had been disturbing, though nothing like as bad as the one that recurred almost nightly, which was so terrifying that she sometimes woke up gasping for breath. Terrifying, not because her imagination was running riot but, on the contrary, because it was in every detail a recollection of real events that Hulda could never, however hard she tried, forget.

Sitting up, she took a deep breath to dispel these phantoms. What she needed now was a cup of good strong coffee.

It occurred to her that she might actually be able to get used to not working. No commitments, no alarm clock. A comfortable if monotonous life as a pensioner in a fourth-floor apartment.

Except she had no intention of getting used to it.

She had to have a purpose in life. In the short term, she needed to solve the case of Elena's death, or at least give it her best shot. She knew a success like that would allow her to leave her job in a cloud of glory, but, more than that, she felt an overwhelming urge to achieve some kind of justice for the poor girl. In the long term, she wanted to settle down with someone, escape the loneliness, and maybe – just maybe – Pétur was the one.

It didn't occur to her to check her phone until she was halfway through her first cup of coffee because, unlike the current smartphone-obsessed generation, she wasn't in thrall to her device. The younger members of CID could scarcely tear themselves away from their screens for a minute, whereas if she had the choice, Hulda would prefer never to have to look at hers at all.

So it came as a surprise that someone should have tried to ring her, twice, from a number she didn't recognize. A call to directory enquiries revealed that the number belonged to the hostel that had featured so prominently in her dreams.

The phone was answered by a young man.

'Good morning, this is Hulda Hermannsdóttir. I'm calling from the police.'

'Right. Morning,' he replied.

'Someone was trying to reach me from this number at about eight o'clock this morning.'

'Oh, yeah? From this number? Could've been Dóra, but then it could have been anyone, really. Wasn't me, though,' he said, running his words together in a barely audible mumble.

'What do you mean by "anyone"?' asked Hulda.

'Well, you know, all the residents have access to this phone.' He qualified this: 'Only for domestic calls, though. International numbers are blocked, or you can bet the phone bill would be sky high.' He laughed.

Hulda was in no laughing mood. 'Is there any way of finding out who called me? Or could you just put me through to Dóra?'

'Dóra? Sorry, no can do.'

'Why not?' Hulda asked, her patience wearing thin. Clearly, half a cup of coffee wasn't enough.

'She was on night shift so she's asleep now. And there's no point bothering her, as she'll have her phone turned off.'

'But this is urgent,' Hulda protested, though for all she knew it might not be. 'Just give me her landline, would you?'

The young man laughed again. 'Landline? No one uses a landline any more.'

'Well, then, can you just ask her to ring me?'

'OK, I'll try and remember. On the number you're calling from now?'

'Yes,' said Hulda, then belatedly remembered something.

'You've got a girl from Syria staying and I need to talk to her. Is she there?'

'Syria? I wouldn't know. I'm new, you see, don't know anyone yet. Dóra would have a better idea.'

Hulda abandoned the struggle. 'Never mind,' she said curtly. 'I'll ring back later.'

'OK. Should I not bother to pass on the message then – about giving you a call?'

'For God's sake, yes, please ask her to ring me. Thank you.'

Hulda hung up with an exasperated sigh and poured herself more coffee.

II

The first day in their new home: a tiny basement flat so small that the word 'flat' was pushing it a bit, but it was a big day, nonetheless.

She had finally, belatedly, moved out of her parents' place, bidding them a fond farewell while silently promising herself never to go back. Next, she had gone to collect her daughter, a little uncertain of her reception or indeed of whether she would be allowed to take her away.

Her worries had proved groundless. The matron in charge had remarked that two years was an unusually long time for the girl to have been living with them: normally, children spent only a few months there. She'd also warned that the change would take her daughter a while to adjust to, but wished them both all the best. She's a good girl, she said.

And, God, it had been tough. The child had howled and howled, refusing to let her mother pick her up, refusing to go with her. This wasn't the reunion the mother had been dreaming of for so long.

When they were finally ready to leave, the matron had added: 'She sometimes has a bit of trouble getting to sleep.'

'Trouble getting to sleep?' the mother had queried. 'Do you have any idea why?'

The matron looked doubtful, apparently wondering how much it would be wise to reveal about the girl's time in their care, but in the end she had reluctantly admitted: 'We had a child staying with us earlier this year who used to' – She hesitated – 'apparently used to amuse himself by poking the other children in the eye while they were sleeping.'

A shiver had run down the mother's spine on hearing this.

'At first, we thought it was a one-off,' the matron had continued, 'but in the end we were forced to intervene. Your daughter's a sensitive child, so it affected her more than most. She's had trouble sleeping ever since; too afraid of the dark to close her eyes. Frankly, it's been a real nuisance.'

That first day, the girl did not take kindly to her new home or to the presence of her mother. She refused to talk and avoided her mother's eye. To begin with, she wouldn't even eat, though she relented in the end. And, inevitably, when evening came, she refused to go to sleep. Lullabies didn't work for long and, in her desperation, the young woman began to wonder if she'd made a terrible mistake. Perhaps she should have given her baby up for adoption straight away instead of settling for this com-promise, which had left her a mother in name only. Now, she was just the woman who had regularly appeared on the other side of a glass screen, trying to think of things to say, mouthing platitudes that could never be a substitute for real love and security.

The little girl couldn't fight off her tiredness for ever, though she did her best. At long last, the mother succeeded in getting her to sleep by leaving a light on in the bedroom. Exhausted, she fell asleep herself immediately afterwards, lying beside her daughter in bed. She had never felt happier than in that moment.

III

Hulda was a little surprised not to have heard from Magnús. After the earful Alexander had given her yesterday evening, she had been expecting a similar call from her boss. There were only two possible explanations for why this hadn't happened: the first was that Magnús had decided to ignore Alexander's complaints and let Hulda get on with investigating the case in peace. Which was highly unlikely, since those two were as thick as thieves and, if Alexander had complained, you could be sure that Magnús would have backed him up. The second, more likely, explanation was that Alexander hadn't run telling tales to Magnús after all, perhaps because he knew deep down that he had screwed up the inquiry. He must be praying that Hulda would fail to dig up any new information so the whole affair could quietly sink without trace. She did wonder how Alexander had known she was looking into Elena's death, but the most likely explanation was that Albert had told him, since they knew each other from Albert's time in the police.

Convenient as Magnús's non-intervention was, Hulda

knew she couldn't rely on it for long. She had been given two weeks' grace to work on the case, but there was a real risk she would be ordered to wrap up her inquiry before that, perhaps with only a day's notice to clear her desk, so it was vital to use her remaining time well. The first task on the agenda was to follow up the lead she'd got from the interpreter, Bjartur. And when it came to the sex industry or human trafficking, the fount of all wisdom in the police was an officer known as Thrándur. He'd actually been christened Tróndur, since he was half Faroese, but as he'd lived in Iceland all his life he usually went by the local version of the name. Hulda had never particularly warmed to the man, though he'd always been perfectly polite to her. His manner struck her as too smarmy, but she had to admit that her opinion of Thrándur and various other male colleagues was bound to be coloured by the fact that she wasn't part of their clique. To give him credit, though, at least Thrándur was a competent detective: he was cautious, intelligent and generally got good results, unlike Alexander.

Thrándur didn't answer his desk phone, so she tried his mobile. It rang for ages until, finally, he picked up.

'Thrándur speaking,' he said formally. To her chagrin, she realized this meant he hadn't bothered to add her number to his contacts list, in spite of all the years they'd worked together.

'Thrándur, it's Hulda here. Could I see you for a quick chat?'

'Why, Hulda! It's been ages,' he said, with a politeness she felt was put on. 'I've got the day off, actually – had to use up a bit of leave left over from last summer. Can it wait until tomorrow?'

She thought for a moment. Time was of the essence: she had to make some sort of progress today and this was the most promising lead she had.

'I'm sorry, it's urgent.'

'OK, fire away.'

'Could I come and see you?' She knew this would be more likely to produce a result: if he lied to her, she'd have a better chance of spotting it from his body language.

'Well, I'm on the golf course.' This didn't surprise her: Thrándur was the police team's star player. 'And I'm about to tee off. Can you be quick?'

'Where are you?'

'Urridavellir.'

This didn't mean anything to her.

'The course up at Heidmörk,' he clarified, when she didn't react. He gave her directions.

'I'll be with you in a minute,' she lied, well aware that her old Skoda wouldn't be up to the challenge.

As she drove south-east out of town, she found her thoughts dwelling on Pétur. On what a good evening they'd had and how much she'd missed that kind of companionship. She also reflected on what she'd told him about her past, and even more on what she'd left unsaid. For now. There would be plenty of time for that later.

Just beyond the outskirts of the city, the Heidmörk Nature Reserve greeted her in all its fresh spring greenery, the conifers, birches and low-lying scrub caught midway between the drabness of winter and their full summer glory. In the ever-expanding concrete jungle of Reykjavík, Heidmörk offered a calm oasis of trees and hiking trails where people could enjoy days out with their families.

Thrándur's directions had been clear, and a long career in the police had taught her to pay attention to details, so the way to the golf course wasn't hard to find. In spite of the tortuous winding of the narrow gravel road that made it impossible to see any oncoming traffic, Hulda and the Skoda made it to their destination in one piece.

Thrándur was standing waiting for her in the car park, dressed up to the nines in a natty golfing costume of diamond-patterned jumper and peaked cap, a trolley and a set of clubs at his side. Hulda had no basis on which to judge his outfit but, given Thrándur's golfing mania, she assumed he would have no truck with anything but the best.

'I'm a bit pressed for time,' he said as she approached, unable to keep a note of impatience out of his voice. As if for emphasis, he glanced over at the large clock on the clubhouse. 'What was it you wanted to discuss?'

Hulda wasn't used to being chivvied but, clearly, Thrándur wasn't prepared to let anything get in the way of his game.

She came straight to the point. 'It's about a Russian girl who died a year ago. Her name was Elena.'

'Doesn't ring any bells, I'm afraid,' he said. 'Wish I could help you.' He was politeness personified, in spite of his evident hurry.

'She came to the country as an asylum-seeker, then turned up dead on a beach on Vatnsleysuströnd. The original investigation was a bit sketchy, but I've just learned that she may have been brought over to work as a prostitute, possibly as part of a trafficking ring.' She kept a close eye on Thrándur's reaction, noting that she had piqued his interest. 'That's why I wanted to talk to you,' she finished.

'I . . . I don't know anything about that,' he said in an altered tone, more hesitant now, and evasive. 'I've never heard of any Elena.' Then, as an afterthought: 'Sorry.'

'It's not unheard of, though, is it?' Hulda persisted. 'For people to come to this country on the pretext of seeking asylum when they're actually part of some kind of organized prostitution network?' She had done some quick research online before coming out and had found enough to justify this assertion, at least for the purpose of probing Thrándur for more information.

'Well, yes, sure, it does happen, I suppose, but it's not something we're looking into at present. It sounds as though you've been given some misleading information.'

'If something like that *was* going on,' Hulda persevered, 'are there any names you could give me; anyone who might be involved in that kind of racket? Anyone based here in Iceland?'

'No one comes to mind,' he replied, a shade too quickly, she thought; without even pausing to think, as if he'd prefer her to stay well away from investigating anything along those lines. 'Maybe it was a one-off: someone brought her to the country then made himself scarce. That's the most likely scenario, don't you think?'

'It's possible,' she said slowly, 'I suppose. Who would be the most likely candidates in that case? If anyone ought to know, it's you.' She was polite but insistent.

'I'm sorry, Hulda,' he said again, 'but I haven't the fog-giest. It's not as straightforward as you seem to think. Fortunately, we don't have much organized crime of that sort in Iceland. Sorry, look, I really do have to go now: if I'm late, I'll miss my tee time.'

She nodded, though the golfing term meant nothing to her. 'Thanks, anyway, Thrándur. It was good to be able to pick your brains.'

'No problem, Hulda. Any time.' Then he added, and she thought she detected a hint of sarcasm in his voice: 'Enjoy your retirement.'

She watched him lugging his golf clubs up the path to a small knoll where three other golfers were standing, evidently waiting for him. It was a lovely day for it. The sky was a pure, cloudless blue: a sight for sore eyes after the dreary winter, though there was still a distinct nip in the air.

It looked as though Thrándur was going to be first to tee off, or whatever it was called. He reached into his bag for a club then, noticing that Hulda was still standing in the car park, watching him, he gave her an awkward smile and paused, waiting for her to leave. She waved back, not budging an inch, enjoying his discomfort. He looked away and took up position, his back to Hulda, club raised aloft like a weapon, then, swinging it back, struck the ball a tremendous clout. It flew off the fairway and landed on the other side of a barbed-wire fence. From the reactions of Thrándur and his companions, she gathered that this had not been the intention.

IV

The girl was still locked in her shell, showing little emotion apart from the constant crying, but her mother refused to give up. The gulf between them had to be bridged somehow. It was as if her daughter was punishing her for her absence, which was terribly unfair because the mother had been powerless to act any differently. She'd had no real choice. And now here she was, alone with her child, hardly able to sleep at night for anxiety about the future. How was she to combine work with bringing up a child on her own? Almost all the women she knew were married housewives, with plenty of time for their homes and children. It wasn't only society that was against her: even these so-called friends didn't hide their disapproval of her status as a single mother. Meanwhile, her parents, still adamant that the little girl should have been given up for adoption, had reacted badly to her decision to go it alone and were keeping their distance. Most days, she felt she had nowhere to turn for help.

Far from being toughened up by adversity, she felt herself being worn down, a little more every day.

When she was at work, the mother had no choice but to entrust her daughter to a childminder who lived nearby, a cold, strict woman with old-fashioned notions about bringing up children. Every weekday, it was a wrench for the mother to leave her little girl in the childminder's stuffy basement flat, which reeked of cigarette smoke. But she had to work, or she wouldn't be able to support herself and her daughter, and this woman offered the only day-care services she could afford in her neighbourhood.

Saying goodbye to her daughter never got any easier. Although she knew she would be collecting her again at the end of the day, each parting seemed a repetition of their original separation. She prayed that the little girl didn't feel the same way. The child wept every time, but it wasn't clear that being parted from her mother was the cause of her tears.

She told herself that everything would be all right in the end, that the relationship between mother and daughter would eventually become normal. Normal was all she asked for. But, deep down, she felt – she knew – that this would never be the case. The damage was irreparable.

V

Thrándur had been withholding information, that much was clear, but Hulda wasn't going to let this deter her. Among her few friends on the force there was one person who had the necessary contacts in the shady world in which Thrándur spent his days.

Since Hulda had absolutely no desire to set foot in CID, she arranged to meet her friend in the café at Kjarvalsstadir, an art gallery just outside the centre of town. The case was certainly keeping her busy. Although she felt a sense of duty towards Elena for some reason, she also knew that the case was a means of deflecting the gut-wrenching sense of rejection that flooded her every time she relived her conversation with Magnús.

There was hardly anyone else in the café apart from a young couple – tourists, judging by their backpacks and camera – who were tucking into slices of apple pie. They were so obviously in love, like her and Jón back in the day. Her heart wasn't easily won, but she had fallen deeply in love with him once and the memory was still painfully vivid. No such powerful emotion stirred in her breast for Pétur, but that was all right: she genuinely liked him and could envisage some sort of future with him. That was enough. She'd probably lost the capacity to love – not just probably; definitely – and she knew precisely the moment at which that had happened.

The apple pie looked so tempting that Hulda ordered a slice while she waited and was just finishing the last mouthful when her friend walked into the gallery café. Karen was twenty years younger than her, but they had always got on well. Hulda had taken her under her wing – not in a maternal way, since she could never have thought of Karen as a daughter, but like a teacher with a pupil. Seeing herself in the younger woman, she had tried to guide her through the labyrinthine world of the police patriarchy. Karen had proved an apt pupil. She was now on a fast track up through the ranks, getting opportunities and positions that Hulda could only have dreamed of. Hulda had watched her protégée's meteoric rise with a pride not unmixed with envy, a little voice inside her asking: why didn't you rise any higher yourself?

It was a question to which she hadn't found a satisfactory answer. No doubt there had been all kinds of contributing factors, including attitudes to women back in the day, but the truth was that she'd always found it difficult to bond with her colleagues, always kept them at arm's length, and had paid the price for that in her career.

'Hulda, hon, how are you? Is it true you're leaving? Have you already left?' Karen slipped into the chair opposite her. 'I'm afraid I can't stay long – rushed off my feet at work, you know how it is.'

Karen used to work for Thrándur in the vice squad, but now she had taken the next step up the ladder.

'Won't you have a coffee?' asked Hulda. 'And some cake?'

'Definitely no cake, I'm gluten free these days, but I'll have a coffee.' Karen stood up again. 'I'll fetch it myself.'

'No, please, let me –'

'No, I won't hear of it,' Karen interrupted, in what sounded to Hulda like a pitying tone. Like one cup of coffee would bankrupt her, now that she was retiring. If there was one thing Hulda couldn't stand, it was being pitied. Still, she wasn't going to waste her time arguing over something this trivial, so she let it go.

'We really must do lunch from time to time,' said Karen, returning with a cappuccino, 'so we don't lose touch. Of course, I knew you were older than me, but I didn't realize you were that old.' Astonishingly, Karen seemed to regard this as a compliment. She beamed, not the least embarrassed by her faux pas. Perhaps she thought Hulda would be flattered by this reference to her youthful appearance.

Hulda tried to shrug off her irritation, but it was dawning on her that they had never really been friends after all. Karen had needed her support and friendship while she was clawing her way up through the hierarchy, but now, clearly, Hulda had served her purpose and could be tossed aside. She silently cursed herself for not having realized this before, but right now she needed Karen.

'I'm retiring,' she said.

'Yes, I heard. We'll all miss you terribly, hon, you know that.'

'Yes, right. Same here,' Hulda said insincerely. 'Anyway, there's a little matter Magnús asked me to clear up before I go; something he needed an experienced officer to cast an eye over.' This was being economical with the truth, but then Hulda was getting used to that.

'Really, did Maggi do that?' Karen sounded unflatteringly surprised.

It would never have occurred to Hulda to refer to her boss as 'Maggi'.

'Yes, he did. It concerns a young Russian woman who died a little over a year ago. She may have been working as a prostitute here, under cover of being an asylum-seeker.'

Karen's face had taken on a vacant look. She glanced at her watch and smiled in a perfunctory way, clearly impatient to be off.

After a short, rather awkward silence, she said: 'Sorry, I don't think I can help you there. I've never heard of the case and, anyway, I've moved on.'

'Yes, I'm aware of that,' Hulda said calmly, 'but I was under the impression that you were quite well informed about that world – familiar with the main names and faces. But maybe I've misunderstood the kind of jobs you were . . .' She left it dangling. It had crossed her mind to ask bluntly if this meant that Karen hadn't been entrusted with anything *important*, but she reckoned she'd got the message across loud and clear.

'No, you were right. Shoot,' said Karen, taking the bait.

'Are there any characters we still haven't managed to nail who are suspected of . . . well, of being in that line of business?'

'I'm not sure what the scene's like today, but there is one candidate who springs to mind. Though . . .' Karen dried up, but Hulda wasn't about to let her off the hook. She waited . . . then waited a little longer: that was one thing she knew how to do. Sure enough, Karen soon felt compelled to continue: 'But it was difficult to pin any-thing on him, so we more or less gave up. His name's Áki Ákason – you may have heard of him. He runs a wholesale business.'

The name was familiar, all right, though Hulda couldn't put a face to it. 'Young or old?'

'About forty. Lives in the west of town, in a flashy house that must have cost a packet.'

'The wholesale business can pay well.'

'Not that well, believe me. He's up to his neck in it. But sometimes you just can't get anything to stick, so you have to let it go and move on. For Christ's sake, don't spread it any further, though; officially, the man's squeaky clean.'

'Don't worry, I'll keep it to myself,' Hulda assured her. 'It's interesting, but I doubt it'll help me directly. What I need is a link to the dead girl.'

'I hear you. Anyway . . .'

And so they parted, with no warmth on either side. In spite of what she had said, Hulda had every intention of paying this wholesaler a visit. After all, what did she have to lose?

VI

Although life with her daughter was settling into a routine, it wasn't quite how the mother had pictured it. She was finding it a hard, unrelenting struggle. The child was naughty, fractious and withdrawn, though the mother did her best to lavish on her all the love and kindness she was capable of. Evenings were the most difficult time: the little girl was still so afraid of the dark that she would only go to sleep with the light on. Their financial situation was precarious, too, and all the worries about her child, about money and the future, were taking their toll.

She had begun to regret that she had never told the girl's father she was carrying his child. He was an American soldier, stationed briefly in Iceland after the war, and their relationship had been even briefer, lasting only a night or two. When she realized she was expecting a baby, she had lain awake night after night, agonizing over whether to look him up, but the barrier had seemed insurmountable. She simply couldn't bring herself to do it, too ashamed of their relationship and what it had led to. Of course, they were both equally to blame for what had happened, but he was free to swan off back to his homeland, leaving her to face the consequences: pregnancy and an illegitimate child; having to look family and friends in the eye.

Now, of course, it was too late. He had gone back to America. Although she knew which state he lived in, that wouldn't help much, since, incredible as it seemed, she didn't know his second name. He must have told her at some point, but her English was limited and she had probably missed it. Besides, it would have seemed irrelevant at the time. If she hadn't been so dreadfully ashamed, she could have got hold of him when she first found out she was pregnant, since he'd still been in Iceland then. But the thought of travelling out to the American base at Keflavík and asking to speak to a soldier, armed with nothing but his Christian name, her belly already beginning to show . . . God, no, she couldn't do it. Yet, now, she could have kicked herself for being so pathetic. She wished she'd brazened it out for the child's sake, for the little girl who'd had such a difficult beginning in life and would probably never get to know her father. And he would never know that he had a beautiful daughter in the cold wastes of Iceland. It had been just one of many postings for the handsome young soldier but, although he may have visited the country only once, he had left behind a permanent reminder of his presence.

She dreaded the thought of having to explain this to her daughter one day.

VII

Hulda was still at Kjarvalsstadir when Dóra from the hostel rang.

'I couldn't get hold of you this morning,' Dóra said. 'Am I interrupting anything?'

After Karen left, Hulda had stayed on in the café, feeling tired and flat. She needed to sit there a little longer before she could summon up the energy to go back outside into the Icelandic spring weather, which, this time, heralded an end rather than a beginning. The fact was she simply couldn't come to terms with the idea of having to give up work. It wasn't only her boss's offhand manner of breaking the news to her that had brought on this state of bemused shock; nor was it only that she was upset about having to leave earlier than planned: she was upset about having to leave at all. Say what you like about her colleagues, their company was a lifeline for her. Even their bickering and envy were preferable to being cooped up within the four walls of her high-rise flat, where, with nothing to distract her, she would be overwhelmed by memories of the past. Not only overwhelmed, but suffocated. She had been a restless sleeper for as long as she could remember, even before the recurrent nightmares had begun. All that kept her going were her cases, her investigations, the pressure of the job. Last night had been typical – the dreams of the dead Russian girl had pushed aside those other, unwanted memories from the past: her regret, her guilt. Could she have done something differently . . . ?

Hulda sat there, brooding on her fate. She was the only person left in the gallery café; even the tourists had gone. No one was interested in Icelandic art or Icelandic apple pie with cream on such a gloriously sunny day, despite the chill northerly breeze. After all, you could always find a sheltered spot outside somewhere.

Was this what all her days would be like once she was pensioned off? Sitting around in cafés, trying to fill the long, empty hours? She toyed with the idea of ringing Pétur and inviting him to join her for a coffee but checked the impulse, not wanting to come across as too keen.

And Dóra asked if she was interrupting anything. The irony.

'No,' said Hulda, telling the simple truth. 'Sorry I didn't hear the phone earlier. I hope it wasn't anything urgent.'

'Oh, no, not at all. To be honest, I can't understand why you're bothering with this. The girl died ages ago and everyone else is satisfied – if you know what I mean.'

Hulda did, only too well. With no one to speak up for her, the poor Russian girl had received shoddy treatment from the police. Although this wasn't her fault, Hulda felt ashamed.

'I just happened to remember something – it's probably totally irrelevant but, you never know, it might be of use to you.'

Instantly, Hulda was on the edge of her seat, ears pricked.

'Only there was some bloke who came to pick her up once – a stranger.'

'A stranger?'

'Yeah, not one of the lawyers who usually handle these asylum cases. Not that Russian interpreter guy either. Someone else.'

'You say he picked her up?'

'Yes, I saw her getting into his car outside the hostel. It's only just come back to me.' From the sound of her voice, Dóra was feeling rather pleased with herself about having new information to impart. 'You see, I remember wondering where she was going with this bloke because, of course, she didn't know any Icelanders.'

'Was he an Icelander?' Hulda asked, pulling out her notebook and jotting down the details. She felt suddenly energized.

'Yes.'

'How do you know? Did you talk to him?'

'What, me? No. I just ran into them outside, though he must have gone in to ask for her at reception. I was on my way in to start my shift or something.'

'How do you know he was an Icelander?' Hulda repeated.

'You can always tell an Icelander: they all look alike – you know what I mean. Typical Icelandic face, Icelandic appearance.'

'Could you describe him?'

'No, it was too long ago.'

'Was he skinny? Overweight?' Hulda sighed privately at the thought of having to prise all the information out of this girl bit by bit.

'Yes, overweight, that's right. Kind of fat, and a bit of a minger, as far as I remember.'

'Not your type, then?' said Hulda.

'God, no. I remember thinking maybe she'd found herself a boyfriend, but they seemed so badly suited – she was attractive, you know, tall and graceful, but he was short and fat.'

'And you'd never seen him before?'

'No, I don't think so.'

'Do you remember when this was?'

'You must be kidding. I can't even remember what I had for breakfast. God, it was just, I don't know, some time before she died,' said Dóra, pointing out the obvious.

'You think it could have been her boyfriend?' From what she had learned during her conversation with Bjartur, Hulda had her own theory about what had been going on, but she wanted to know if a similar suspicion had struck Dóra. She didn't ask straight out, though. There was no call to start a rumour – not yet, anyway.

'Well, no, not really, it just crossed my mind. If she'd had an Icelandic boyfriend, I'm sure he'd have been much fitter than this bloke.'

'Can you think what business he might have had with her?'

'No. But then it was nothing to do with me. I have enough on my plate with running this place; what the residents get up to isn't my problem.'

'What sort of age was he?'

'Hard to say. He was just a bloke. Sort of middle-aged, you know. Older than her.'

'Did you see what kind of car he was driving?'

'Hey, yeah, a big off-roader. Blokes like him all drive four-by-fours like that; black ones, usually.'

'What kind of four-by-four?'

'Don't ask me, I can't tell them apart. They all look the same.'

'Could this have been the day she died?'

'You know, I'm not sure,' Dóra said. 'It might have been the day before, but I doubt it. Surely I'd have connected the two things at the time?'

'I wouldn't know,' Hulda pointed out.

'No, right.'

'Have you seen the man again since?'

'No, I don't think so.'

'This is all very interesting, Dóra. Thanks for ringing. Could you get back in touch if you remember anything else? Anything at all.'

'Yeah, sure. This is kind of fun, isn't it? This detective game. I mean, I sometimes read crime novels, but I never thought I'd get mixed up in a case myself.'

'It's not quite the same thing,' Hulda began in a dampening tone, then, spying an opening, changed her tune and added in a more encouraging voice: 'But could you do me a favour and keep your eyes peeled at your end?'

'How do you mean?'

'Ask around, in case anyone remembers a detail that might be important. You see, I believe Elena was murdered, and it's up to us to try and find the person responsible.' She experienced a twinge of doubt: could she be putting this girl in a compromising position – in danger, even . . . ? She dismissed the idea. That's not how things worked in a peaceful little place like Iceland. Here, people killed only once: on the spur of the moment; under the influence of alcohol or drugs; in a fit of rage or jealousy. Premeditated murder was unheard of, let alone someone committing more than one killing of that type. She was on the trail of a murderer, all right, she had no doubt of that, but Dóra was safe.

'Sure. I'll ask around, no problem.'

'What happened about the Syrian woman?' Hulda asked. 'Could I maybe talk to her now?'

'No, sorry, you can't. The police came and took her away.'

'What do you mean?'

'She's being deported. It happens. You know, it's a bit like those games of musical chairs you play as a kid. The music starts, everyone gets up and walks in a circle and, when the music stops, one of the chairs is taken away and someone's unlucky. Today, it was the Syrian woman's turn.'

VIII

She had mentioned once or twice that she'd love to get out of town and see a bit more of Iceland. Get out into the countryside, away from the city — not that there was much of a city here. Even Reykjavík was hardly more than a village, compared with what she was used to.

She had only been half serious when she brought up the idea of the trip, never expecting anything to come of it, especially not in this inhospitable weather. A relentless icy gale blew off the sea, day in, day out, accompanied sometimes by rain, more often by snow. The pristine whiteness was beautiful when seen from the window, but the constantly changing conditions meant it seldom kept its postcard prettiness for long, turning first to grey slush, then to ice in the inevitable frosts that followed, before being covered again by a fresh fall of snow.

So it came as a surprise when he rang to suggest a short weekend trip, to see the snow, as he put it. She glanced out of the window at the driving rain, heard the howling of the wind through the glass, and shivered. But you only live once, she thought. Better to agree and experience something new, an adventure on the edge of the Arctic.

'Won't it be cold?' she asked. 'It looks so chilly out there.'

'Colder than this,' he replied, adding, as if he had read her mind: 'It'll be an adventure.'

So they were thinking along the same lines.

She heard herself say yes. But she had other questions, too: where are we going? How will we get there? What shall I bring?

He told her to relax. They'd be going in his four-by-four. Not that they'd be travelling far: the weather was unpredictable and they didn't want to take any chances. Just far enough to get away from it all, to give her a taste of the wilderness.

She tried again: 'Where are we going?'

He wouldn't say.

'You'll see,' he answered at last, then asked if she had a warm coat she could bring, like a down jacket. When she said she had nothing suitable, he offered to lend her one. She would need to get hold of some thick woollen underwear as well, to keep her warm on the journey, especially at night: that's when the cold would really kick in.

For an instant, she wondered if she should change her mind about going, but she felt the pull, the appeal to her spirit of adventure. She told him, as he must already know, that she didn't own any woollen underwear, and he offered to buy her some, to lend her the money. She could pay him back later.

IX

Was it possible that she was closing in on the truth? Was it possible that this unknown man had picked Elena up the day before her body was found; that he'd been a client? Hulda could picture the scene as if she'd been there herself. Could imagine how alone and abandoned Elena must have been feeling, forced into prostitution in an alien land. Perhaps he was her first client. Perhaps, when it came to it, she had said no. Could her refusal have cost her her life?

The idea filled Hulda with impotent rage and hatred. She would have to watch herself. What was it that Bishop Vídalín once wrote? *Rage kindles an inferno in the eyes*; a feeling she knew only too well.

Deciding that this merited another phone call to Bjartur, she rang and asked if Elena had ever referred to any clients – by name or occupation, for example. Bjartur was eager to help but said that, sadly, Elena hadn't shared any details with him.

The next step was to go and see Áki, the businessman

suspected of operating a prostitution ring. Having tracked down his address, Hulda drove over to the upmarket area in the west of town where he lived. His house turned out to be an old single-storey detached villa with a well-kept garden. The branches of the trees were still bare, but there was a sense of expectancy about them, as if they were poised to put out the first buds of spring. An aura of peace hung over the unassuming house in the expensive neighbourhood, as if nobody was home, an impression supported by the absence of a car on the drive. She tried the doorbell, but got no reply, so she decided to wait for a while in her car, in case the owner returned. This was the best tip she had received so far and she wanted to ambush Áki in person, bombard him with questions before he had a chance to prepare his replies. Besides, she had nowhere else to go. Backing up a little, she parked the old Skoda at a discreet distance, in a spot where she still had a good view of the house.

She'd lost count of the hours she'd spent waiting in her car during her career – it had the comfort of long habit – but by the time two hours had passed she was itching to stand up and stretch her legs. Best stick it out a bit longer, she told herself. Or should she knock on the door on the off-chance? After all, he might be in; he might have been home all day.

As she was weighing up her options, a four-by-four pulled into the drive. Out stepped a lean, youngish-looking man with cropped hair and a brisk, decisive manner. Hulda watched him enter the house and gave it a couple of minutes before following in his footsteps and knocking on the door. The man answered it himself, still in his outdoor shoes and jacket.

He seemed surprised by the visit and waited, still and watchful, for her to state her business.

'Áki?' Hulda did her best to sound calm and collected.

He nodded, his lips twitching in a rather charming smile.

'Could I have a word?'

'That depends. What about?' His voice was soft, with a hint of firmness underneath.

'My name's Hulda Hermannsdóttir. I'm with the police.' She reached into her pocket, hoping her ID was there.

'The police,' he said pensively. 'I see. You'd better come in. Has something happened?'

She wanted to say yes, recalling the photographs of Elena's body on the beach, but stopped herself: 'No, nothing like that. I'm just making a few inquiries, if that's all right with you.' She was as polite as she could be in the circumstances, unwilling to give Áki any reason to call his solicitor. Better keep things simple for the time being. It would be difficult to justify this visit on the basis of the evidence currently available to her. Just prod him a little and see what happened, try to get a sense of what he was like.

He offered her a seat in the living room – possibly one of several, since the house seemed larger inside than it had appeared from the outside. The decor was modern and minimalist, the colour scheme dominated by monochrome and steel. Hulda took a seat on a black sofa made of some shiny material that felt icy to the touch, while Áki perched facing her on a footstool, part of a set with a handsome armchair.

'I'm a bit pushed for time, actually,' was his opening comment, as if to mark his territory, convey the message that she was only there on his terms.

'Me, too,' she said, conscious that her days as a police officer were numbered. 'I wanted to ask you about a young woman from Russia . . .' She allowed a brief silence to develop, in which she studied Áki's reaction and thought she detected signs that he knew what she was talking about. His gaze flickered away for a second then locked with hers again.

'Russia?'

'She came to Iceland as an asylum-seeker,' Hulda elaborated, deciding to plunge straight in without giving him any warning, 'but it seems likely she was actually a victim of sex trafficking.' This was the theory she was working on, so she might as well go ahead and state it as a fact.

'I'm afraid I have no idea what you're talking about, Hulda.' His gaze remained locked with hers. 'I'm not with you at all. Are you under the impression that I know this woman?'

Know, in the present tense. A sign that he knew nothing about Elena and what had happened to her, or that he was guilty and trying to throw her off the scent?

'She's dead,' Hulda stated bluntly. 'Her name was Elena. Her body turned up in a cove on Vatnsleysuströnd.'

Áki's face remained expressionless.

But he didn't seem about to show Hulda the door. He sat tight: self-possessed, outwardly respectable, in dark-blue jeans, white shirt, black leather jacket and shiny black shoes. His entire appearance, like his house and car, signalled affluence.

'Nice house, by the way,' Hulda remarked, surveying her surroundings. 'What do you do for a living?'

'Thanks. Though my wife deserves most of the credit. We enjoy being surrounded by beautiful things.'

Hulda smiled. 'Beautiful' wasn't the first word that sprang to mind when she saw the furniture and interior decor; 'soulless' was the adjective she'd have chosen.

But she didn't say anything, merely waited for him to answer her question.

'I'm in the wholesale business,' he said after a moment, clearly proud of the fact, or at least keen to give that impression.

'What do you sell?'

'What do you want?' His smile widened, then he went on, more soberly: 'Maybe I shouldn't joke about it in front of a cop. I import a bit of this and a bit of that: alcohol, furniture, electrical goods, whatever can be sold on for a good margin. I hope being a capitalist isn't a crime yet.'

'Of course not. And that's it?'

'It?'

'Were you acquainted with Elena at all? I can show you a photo of her.'

'There's no need. I can assure you I didn't know her. I've never heard her name before, never met any Russian asylum-seekers, don't do any business with Russia full stop. And I'm happily married, so I have no need to resort to hookers, if that's what you're implying.' He still exuded an almost preternatural calm.

'No, far from it,' Hulda assured him. She was aware of a growing sense of unease, in spite of the opulent surroundings. The glass coffee table between them shone like a mirror, the room was light and airy, the late-afternoon sun sent shafts of light through the windows. Áki gave the impression of being a perfectly respectable member of the public, polite, well groomed, good-looking even, yet her gut instinct told her she was crossing swords with a formidable adversary – and on his home ground.

Although the ensuing silence lasted only a few seconds, the time seemed to pass with infinite slowness.

'Actually, what I wanted to ask . . .' Unusually for her, Hulda was hesitant. She forced herself to continue: 'What I wanted to ask is whether you were responsible for bringing her to the country.'

Áki didn't seem remotely disturbed.

'Well, there's a question. Are you asking me if I brought a prostitute into the country?'

'Yes, or prostitutes.'

'Now you've really lost me.' His voice had acquired a slight edge, and Hulda felt suddenly, unaccountably, chilled, despite the warmth of the room.

'I'm talking about trafficking,' she went on doggedly. 'Organized prostitution. According to my information, Elena was mixed up in that kind of racket.'

'Interesting. And why exactly would you think that I'm

involved in that line of business?' Áki's voice had recovered its silky smoothness.

'I don't think anything,' Hulda said hastily, reluctant to accuse him directly of being engaged in criminal activities when she had no solid evidence.

'But you're insinuating as much,' he said, smiling again.

'No, I'm simply asking if you know anything about this girl or that kind of activity?'

'And I've already told you that I don't. To be frank, I find it a bit much that a police officer should come knocking on the door of a law-abiding citizen like me, someone who's always paid more than his fair share of tax, and coolly accuse me of running some kind of vice ring. Don't you agree?' He was still oddly calm, his voice level. Hulda wondered if an innocent man wouldn't have been more affronted, more self-righteously angry.

'I haven't accused you of anything, and if you know nothing about Elena . . .'

'Why did you come here?' he asked abruptly, catching her off guard. 'What gave you the idea to come and see me?'

She could hardly tell him that her source in the police believed him to be a major player in the sex industry.

After an awkward pause, she said: 'An anonymous tip-off.'

'An anonymous tip-off? They're not always reliable, are they?' He pressed home his advantage: 'Have you got any evidence for me to refute? It's hard to defend yourself against allegations snatched from thin air. You must be aware' – he leaned a little closer – 'that I have a reputation to protect. In business, a good reputation is everything.'

'I quite understand. And I can assure you that this conversation won't go any further. Since you're obviously unfamiliar with the case, there's nothing more to be said.' Hulda felt an urgent desire to get out of the house, out into the sunny spring afternoon, though Áki's behaviour had not been in the least threatening. Quite the opposite, in fact.

Suddenly, she felt hemmed in. Her palms were sweating and she was feeling increasingly jumpy, sensing that the tables had been turned. She had often tried to enter the heads of suspects, not out of sympathy for their plight so much as to improve her interrogation technique. Over the years, she reckoned she'd become pretty adept at it. Once she had gone so far as to have herself locked in a cell to find out what that sort of confinement felt like and how long she would be able to stick it out. Before locking the door, her colleague had asked if she was sure about this, and she had nodded, despite feeling the cold sweat prickling her skin. He had closed the door, leaving Hulda alone with nothing but the four walls. Next to the reinforced door was a narrow window and, above the bed, another, slightly larger one with frosted glass, the only purpose of which was to admit a small amount of light. Finding herself breathing unnaturally quickly, Hulda had closed her eyes to distract her attention from the fact that she was trapped in a small space. But far from helping, this had made her feel so claustrophobic that she was afraid she was going to faint. Yet she knew that, unlike real prisoners, all she had to do was knock on the door to be let out. Panting, close to hysteria, she had stuck it out for as long as she could before finally jumping up and banging on the door. When her colleague didn't immediately respond, she had been on the verge of screaming, flinging herself against the door and hammering on it with all her might. But at that moment, mercifully, it had opened. She had felt as though she'd been locked in for hours, but her colleague had glanced at the clock and said: 'You only lasted a minute.'

The claustrophobia wasn't as intense now, but something about this encounter in Áki's living room had triggered the memory.

She rose to her feet. 'It was nice to meet you. Thanks for agreeing to see me unannounced like this.'

Áki stood up as well. 'My pleasure, Hulda. Do get in touch if I can assist you any further with your inquiries.' He extended his hand and she shook it in parting. 'Of course, I'll get in contact if I hear anything,' he said with a laugh. 'Though it's rarely that exciting in the wholesale business. Hulda – Hulda Hermannsdóttir, wasn't it?' he said, and this time there was no mistaking the menace underlying his words.

X

The day of the trip had arrived. She stood to one side, watching him pack two rucksacks, one of them for her. 'Do I really need all that?' she asked, as it dawned on her that this trip was going to be a lot tougher than she had realized. Nodding, he told her she couldn't get away with any less kit. The pack contained a sleeping bag that would keep her alive during the freezing nights, food supplies, a thick scarf, a pair of gloves that looked too big for her, a woolly hat and an empty bottle. When she asked if she should fill it with water, he laughed. Don't forget we're in Iceland: there's more than enough clean water here. We'll be staying overnight in a mountain hut and the water in the stream there is far purer than anything you'll get out of the tap.

Just when she thought there wasn't room for anything else, he had added a torch and some batteries then announced that he reckoned that was it. She lifted her pack with difficulty, gasping at the weight and exclaiming that it was far too heavy. 'Nonsense,' he said. 'You won't notice it once it's on your back. You'll need these, too . . . He reached for a pair of walking poles and strapped them to the outside.

After loading both packs into the car, he asked if she knew how to ski. She shook her head, spotting a ray of light, a possible way out. She'd never skied in her life, she told him, and it was far too late to start now. Perhaps they'd better not go on the trip after all. He laughed and said there was no way he was going to let her down like that. Then he disappeared and returned with a pair of skis, two poles and a thick rope.

She asked nervously if he was planning to go skiing without her.

It was a safety precaution, he explained: if anything went wrong he could ski for help. Seeing her eyes on the rope, he added that it was necessary in case the car got bogged down.

'Are you expecting that to happen?' she asked, her breath catching in her throat.

'No, no chance,' he reassured her. And she believed him.

She climbed into the passenger seat and he switched on the ignition, then suddenly appeared to remember something. Telling her to hang on a minute, he hurried back inside, leaving the engine running. She watched him in the mirror and, when she saw him return, carrying two axes, her heart missed a beat. He shoved them in the boot and got back behind the wheel.

'Were those . . . axes?' Her voice trembled a little, though she did her best to hide the chill that had flooded her heart at the sight.

'Sure, ice axes — one each.'

'Why on earth do we need ice axes?' she asked. 'I don't want to take any risks: I'm not used to extreme sports.'

'Don't worry, they're just a precaution. It's better to be prepared for every eventuality. It won't be dangerous, just an adventure.'

Just an adventure.

XI

Hulda had a clear memory of the day Jón died.

She had been working late, as she often did, looking into a violent attack in the centre of Reykjavík. She wasn't officially in charge of the case, but she had borne most of the weight of the investigation. Incidents like this were fairly frequent at weekends, when the bars were open until late. When they closed, everyone poured out into the streets, creating a carnival atmosphere every Friday and Saturday night. With so many people drunk, the police often had to intervene, and sometimes the cases were serious, leading to formal charges.

It was a Thursday, and Hulda had spent the week interviewing witnesses and trying to establish who had attacked the young man in question, who was still in hospital.

It was nearly midnight when she got back to their house on Álftanes.

A house, but no longer a home.

The couple hardly spoke to each other any more.

Everything about the house felt cold and bleak, from

the trees outside to the atmosphere indoors, the furniture, even the bed. She and Jón no longer shared a room.

She came in to find Jón lying on the living-room floor, so very still, so very dead.

When, in due course, the ambulance arrived, the paramedics had pretended at first that something could be done, trotting out meaningless phrases in an attempt to comfort her, but of course it was too late. He had passed away earlier that day.

'He had a heart condition,' was all Hulda had said. Two colleagues from the police arrived at the scene, young men. She knew them both, though they weren't friends. She didn't have any friends in the police. She had gone to the hospital in the ambulance, staying close by Jón's side.

Since that evening, she had been alone in the world.

XII

She wasn't entirely sure why he had invited her on this trip.

Most of the time he was nice, though there was an intensity about him that made her a little uncomfortable. But he had told her they were friends, and she could really use a friend in this strange country.

She had the feeling he wanted more than just friendship, though; that he harboured stronger feelings for her, but she knew that nothing would ever happen between them.

She had almost turned down his invitation to go on a trip out of town, but decided in the end to embrace this chance to enjoy life a little. She was fairly confident he wouldn't make a move; tried to convince herself he was simply doing her a favour.

After all, what was the worst that could happen?

XIII

The mother had lost her job, not that this should have come as any surprise. Her boss had been dubious about her being a single mother from the first, telling her bluntly that he preferred to employ childless women: they were more reliable and could keep their mind on the job.

Then, one day, he informed her that she needn't bother coming in the next day. She protested that she had a right to a longer period of notice, but he disputed this, denying that he owed her a króna more than he'd already paid her. The following days had been a nightmare, as her worries had proved infectious, making her daughter even more fractious than usual. She calculated how long they could survive on her small pot of savings, how long they'd have enough to eat, how long it would be before they were thrown out of the flat she was renting. The answers didn't look good, however many times she did the sums.

Which was how she ended up swallowing her pride and moving back in with her parents, this time with their grandchild in tow. The old couple quickly came to dote on the child, though their behaviour towards their daughter was cold to begin with. The little girl grew especially close to her grandfather, who would read to her and play with her, but it was as if this caused the fragile bond between mother and daughter to fray, to slowly unravel, until the terrible day when her daughter stopped calling her *Mamma*.

XIV

It was still fairly light when they set off. Once they had left town, the traffic thinned out until, eventually, they turned off on to a sideroad that appeared to be little used. A chain with a sign in the middle had been strung across it, as if to block it off to vehicles.

She turned to look at him and asked if the road was closed.

Nodding, he swung the wheel, swerving off the road then back on to it, on the other side of the chain.

'Is it safe?' she asked nervously. 'Are we allowed to drive on it if it's closed?'

He replied that the road wasn't exactly closed; the sign was just there as a warning that it was impassable.

Again, she experienced that creeping feeling of misgiving, that it was a bad idea to have come on this trip.

'Impassable?' She kept her eyes fixed on his face.

'Don't worry,' he said, patting the wheel and smiling at her. 'Give this baby a chance to show us what she can do.'

In contrast to the bleak, wintry world outside, it was warm in the car, the heater pumping in a constant blast of hot air. She thought about her parents' car back home. The heater had never worked.

She looked out at the landscape, at the vast, treeless expanse, enchanted but a little afraid. Everything was so white, as far as the eye could see, apart from the odd glimpse of black — rocks, perhaps, or tufts of grass. A faint blue light hung over the mountains; the beauty was all-encompassing. It was so peaceful, too. Although they hadn't been driving long, they might have been alone in the world. The isolation was thrilling, yet at the same time it frightened her. The landscape felt somehow cruel and unforgiving, especially now, in winter; nature didn't care if you lived or died. It would be terrifyingly easy to get lost here.

Abruptly, she was jolted out of her thoughts as the car skidded in the deep snow and, for one horrible moment, she thought they were going to veer off the road and roll over. Heart pounding, she braced herself for the impact. But her fears proved unnecessary, as the car righted itself.

The radio was emitting a flow of words that she couldn't understand. It sounded like a monotonous recital of facts.

In the end, she felt compelled to ask what the announcer was saying.

'It's the weather forecast,' her companion replied.

'So what's the forecast like?'

'Not too good,' he said. 'They're predicting a heavy snowfall.'

'Shouldn't we . . .' She hesitated, then said it: 'Shouldn't we turn back, then?'

'No way,' he replied. 'Bad weather will just add to the thrill.'

XV

When her phone rang, Hulda was standing by the hot-dog stand on Tryggvagata, grabbing a quick snack in the evening sun. This particular stand had been an important landmark in Icelandic cuisine for decades. Long before the concept of the takeaway was introduced to the country, its hot dogs had taken on the status of a national dish. Later, the stand had been given the international seal of approval when a former US president had stopped there for a hot dog while on a visit.

She couldn't stop thinking about her conversation with Áki, though it was clear that he was nothing like the description of the man in the four-by-four who, according to Dóra, had picked Elena up.

A pity, as it would have been so handy, establishing a link with Elena and moving the case along.

She tried to answer her mobile without dropping her hot dog or spilling Coke, mustard, ketchup or remoulade down her jacket, a juggling act she had perfected through long practice. Hulda had been patronizing this van for years. It had always been popular but, recently, the queue had grown appreciably longer, thanks to the massive increase in tourist numbers. A crowd of them were now milling around it, either waiting to be served or struggling to eat their own hot dogs without dripping the contents down their fronts.

'Hulda – Albert Albertsson here.' The solicitor's voice was as mellifluous as ever, inspiring trust from the first word, and for an instant Hulda let herself be lulled into believing that he had good news for her: surely a man with a voice like that couldn't be the bearer of bad tidings?

'Hello, Albert.'

'How are you getting on with the . . . investigation?'

'Reasonably well, thanks.'

'Great. I thought I'd give you a bell because I've come across some paperwork relating to Elena. It was in my "filing cabinet" here at home.' Hulda thought she detected a hint of irony when Albert mentioned the filing cabinet and, remembering the chaos in his office, guessed he'd found the papers at the bottom of some pile. But this was good news: additional documents might contain further clues, and she could do with some of those right now.

'Excellent,' she said.

'I've got to go out to Litla-Hraun Prison tomorrow morning to meet a client, but I can take the papers to the office with me in the afternoon. Would you like to drop by then?'

Hulda thought for a moment. 'No, I'll come and pick them up now, if that's OK. Did you say you were at home?'

'Yes, I am, but I'm on my way out – I'm already late, in fact. Though if you're in that much of a hurry, I suppose my brother could give you the paperwork. He lives with me. I'll leave the envelope with him.'

'Great. Where do you live?'

He gave her his address then asked again how the inquiry was progressing and if she really believed Elena had been murdered.

'I'm convinced,' Hulda told him, and rang off.

The evening was still young. Getting hold of the papers wasn't quite as urgent as she'd led him to believe, but she felt a desperate need to keep herself busy. Anything was better than going home alone and trying in vain to get to sleep in the knowledge that she was one day closer to retirement, one day closer to the aching void of enforced inactivity that was all she had to look forward to.

XVI

Suddenly, she shivered, in spite of the heat in the car. She felt instinctively that she shouldn't be here, that she had made a mistake in coming. Nothing concrete had happened to trigger this feeling, yet she found herself breathing unnaturally fast. Maybe it was the inhuman emptiness, the vastness of the landscape, the obliterating blankness of the snow?

'Do you enjoy living here?' she asked, to counter the incipient feeling of panic.

'Of course,' he replied: 'Or at least I think I do. Though, having said that, the weather can be a bit tricky and we don't get too many days of summer, but I sort of enjoy the cold, the snow. Maybe you can understand that, as a Russian?'

She just nodded.

'I think you'll learn to like it,' he added, his voice friendly.

He was being nice to her; she shouldn't be scared of him.

Of course, really, she was scared about her own future, about getting permission to stay in Iceland and what would happen if she didn't.

She tried to relax, to breathe normally. She could worry about the future tomorrow, today she was determined to enjoy the trip. Everything would be just fine.

XVII

It was late summer, over a year after Jón had died.

Hulda was standing on top of Esja, the long, flat-
topped mountain that reared up on the northern side of
Faxaflói bay from Reykjavík. It wasn't a very difficult hike
– she was used to more challenging climbs in the highlands – but it was one she always enjoyed. It was close
enough to the city that you could go there after work in
the long, light evenings of spring and summer, and the
brisk walk up the mountain took well under an hour.

She'd been feeling off-colour all day at work and had
decided to go out and climb the mountain by herself. Of
course, there were other hikers up there, but she was in
her own private world, breathing in the fresh mountain
air and taking in the amazing views of what felt like the
whole south-western corner of Iceland, from the urban
sprawl of Reykjavík across the bay, to the Reykjanes peninsula beyond it to the south and a great tract of the
uninhabited highlands and ice caps to the east.

It was getting late, and she knew she had to start down

again soon, but she wanted to postpone the moment as long as possible. Here, she was in her element; here, she could almost forget everything else. Almost.

But she knew that when she got home and fell asleep, the nightmares would close in again and she would be haunted as always by the same question: *Should I have known?*

XVIII

In the rear-view mirror, she caught a gleam of the low evening sun – or perhaps it was still the afternoon sun, peeping through the clouds. Evening came early in Iceland at this time of year, though they still had a little breathing space before darkness closed in.

The snow covering the road grew deeper and deeper until, finally, the moment she had dreaded arrived: the car got stuck in a drift, wheels spinning, engine screaming. He switched off the ignition, telling her not to worry; she should grab the chance to get out and stretch her legs. It was a relief to escape the overheated, stuffy atmosphere and fill her lungs with great draughts of pure, icy mountain air. Just as well he'd provided her with suitably warm clothes, so the intense cold was invigorating rather than painful.

She took a few tentative steps back and forth, staying close to the car, hesitant at first to step off the road, for fear of what the terrain might be like underneath the smooth, white surface. Seeing this, he grinned at her and gestured to indicate that it was perfectly safe. The snow crunched underfoot and the tracks she left behind were the only ones marring its perfection; the snow was hers and hers alone. As far as the eye could see, there was no other sign of humans, only the empty landscape stretching to the horizon. They were completely alone out here. But her initial apprehension had worn off. What was the worst that could happen?

She watched as he released some air from the tyres to lower the pressure and increase their surface area then jumped back into the driver's seat and started easing the four-by-four out of the drift, inch by inch, until, finally, it was free. At almost the same moment, the first feather-light flakes of snow began to float down and land, ever so gently, on the sleeves of her coat.

XIX

On the day the little girl's grandfather first raised the subject, Reykjavík was basking in unaccustomed sunshine. The mother was standing in a sheltered spot in the yard behind the house, watching her daughter play. The girl made a charming sight in the sunlight, happily absorbed in her game. Perhaps it was unfair to describe such a young child as unhappy, but she rarely looked contented like this.

The proposal knocked the mother sideways, coming as it did from her father, of all people, who had formed such a close relationship with his grandchild. From his voice, she thought perhaps his heart wasn't in it, that he was only echoing the sentiments of the girl's grandmother, who had shown nothing but disapproval from the start. She had left them in no doubt about her opinion that it wasn't desirable for anyone to give birth to a bastard, however endearing the child turned out to be. It brought shame on the whole family – not only on the mother but on her parents as well.

As they stood in that sunny spot in the yard, the grand-father had tentatively suggested having the little girl fostered, maybe even adopted. He knew of a couple out east who were in a position to give her everything she needed, ensuring her a much better life than she could look forward to here in Reykjavík. Good people, he had said, but his voice lacked conviction. Perhaps they weren't good, or perhaps it was the idea itself that wasn't a good one. Nevertheless, his daughter listened, aware how hard it would be for her to say no to the man who had given them a roof over their heads. She couldn't support herself and her daughter on her own; she had failed at the first attempt and needed more time to save up before she could try again.

As the tears welled up in her eyes, she had promised to think about it.

XX

The lawyer's house in the leafy suburb of Grafarvogur reminded Hulda a little of her old home on Álftanes. Though the neighbourhood was very different in character, there was something about the house itself that triggered a rush of nostalgia – the cosy, old-world air, perhaps. Not that it took much to set her off at the moment. Since receiving notice of her dismissal, her thoughts had been turning to the past with unusual frequency. Her budding relationship with Pétur had stirred things up, too, making her uneasily aware of all that she hadn't yet told him.

She rang the doorbell and waited.

Though the man who answered the door was a much shorter, stockier figure than Albert, the family resemblance was unmistakeable. He appeared to be considerably older than his brother, maybe as much as a decade, Hulda guessed, and much thicker about the waist.

'You must be Hulda,' the brother said, smiling; his voice with its smooth radio announcer's tones also giving away his relationship to Albert.

'That's right.'

'Come in.' He led her into a sitting room crowded with mismatched furniture, most of it deeply unfashionable to Hulda's admittedly limited eye for such things. Taking pride of place was a boxy old television set with a large, extremely comfortable-looking recliner planted in front of it.

'I'm Baldur Albertsson, Albert's brother.'

Albert and Baldur: their parents obviously hadn't leafed very far through the book of baby names before plumping for those two, Hulda thought. Next moment, she was struck by a fact she should have noticed straight away: Albert's brother was a perfect match for the description Dóra had given of the man in the four-by-four – short and fat. She caught her breath, at the same time telling herself to get a grip. What was the likelihood that the lawyer's brother could be the man she was after? Admittedly, he had a connection to the case, but only an indirect one. And, anyway, Dóra's vague description could refer to any number of people. Still, it wouldn't hurt to use this opportunity to ask the man a few questions. She toyed with the idea of asking him straight out if he had ever picked Elena up from the hostel, but something told her this would be jumping the gun. Better to let Dóra identify him first, then put him on the spot.

Recalling how jumpy she had felt in Áki's house, Hulda reflected on the contrast now. In spite of her awakening suspicions, Baldur Albertsson continued to come across as an affable, unthreatening presence.

'I gather Albert's not in,' she said, in an attempt at small talk.

'No, he's at a meeting. Always on the go.'

'Are you a lawyer, too?'

Baldur gave a polite chuckle. It had a well-rehearsed sound. Doubtless, it was a question he was often asked. 'Good Lord, no. That's Albert's area – the first and only lawyer in the family. I . . . I'm between jobs at present.'

'I see,' said Hulda, and waited, knowing from experience that direct questions were often unnecessary.

'Albert very generously lets me stay with him,' Baldur elaborated, then, after a brief pause, corrected himself: '"Stay"'s probably the wrong word: I live here, have done for the last two years, ever since I lost my job. This used to be our parents' house, but Albert bought the place off them when they downsized.'

Hulda took a moment to respond to this, trying to think of a diplomatic answer. 'That sounds like a good arrangement . . . assuming you get on well together.'

'Oh, yes, that's never been a problem.' Changing the subject, he asked: 'Would you like a coffee?'

Hulda nodded. She wasn't about to pass up on the opportunity to get to know this man a little better, if there was even an outside chance that he was mixed up in the case. Anyway, he gave the impression of being more in need of company than caffeine.

There was a lengthy interval before he returned with the coffee, which, after all that, turned out to be undrinkable. Never mind, it provided the perfect excuse for a longer chat.

While she was waiting, Hulda had used the time to hunt around the room for a picture of Baldur. She needed one to show Dóra and had thought of using the camera on her phone to take a shot of any photo she found, though the quality wouldn't have been very good, given the knackered state of her mobile. To her frustration, there were none. She wondered if she could surreptitiously snap a picture of him without rousing his suspicions but knew this would tax her agility. She was all fingers and thumbs with her phone and taking a photo required pressing too many buttons.

They sat on either side of a large dining table, and Hulda reflected on how much she would rather have spent this time with Pétur. Then again, maybe it wasn't too late: there was no real distinction between day and night at this time of year; night was nothing more than a state of mind. Thinking about Pétur brought with it the dawning realization that maybe she'd had enough of work after all; there might be something to be said for unlimited evenings off, with no distractions, either direct or indirect, from her job. She was far too inclined to take work home with her, even when there was no need for it. Her mind was always in overdrive. She had never been able to tear herself away from her cases, to switch off completely. Jón used to complain about that, but it was simply how she was made.

'Delicious coffee,' she lied. 'I can only stay for a minute, though. There's somewhere else I've got to be.' She took a sip.

'I tried once,' Baldur remarked. 'To join the police, I mean. Didn't get in.' He patted his impressive paunch. 'Never been in good enough shape, and it's too late to do anything about that now. Albert was always the skinny one.'

There was no hint of resentment in Baldur's words, though this was the second time he had praised his brother at his own expense: earlier, he had mentioned that Albert had been the first in the family to qualify as a lawyer. His admiration of his brother appeared genuine, free from all envy.

'Is he older or younger than you?' Hulda asked tactfully, although the answer was obvious.

'He's ten years younger, as I'm sure you can tell. He was an afterthought – a nice surprise for our parents.'

'Does he handle a lot of these cases?'

'Which ones?'

'Representing asylum-seekers.'

'Yes, I think so. For him, the human rights angle's more important than the money.'

'Presumably he gets paid, though.'

'Yes, of course, but he's mainly in it for the people. He wants to help.'

'What did you do?' Hulda risked a third sip of coffee, but it was so bitter that she discreetly pushed the cup away.

'Do?'

'For a living. Before you moved here. Before losing your job.'

At that moment, Hulda's phone interrupted with a noisy ringing and vibrating on the table beside her cup. She sighed inwardly when she saw that it was Magnús, the last person she wanted to speak to right now. For a moment, she dithered over whether to answer, then decided it could wait. Unsure how to turn off the volume mid-ring, or if that was even possible, she cut the call, seizing the opportunity while she was fumbling with the phone to activate the camera. It required a bit of fiddling, but she hoped Baldur wouldn't cotton on. She pressed 'Capture', and the resulting click seemed to echo around the room. Shooting her companion an apologetic look, she said: 'Sorry, I'm hopeless with this thing. I was trying to switch it to mute.'

'I know what you mean. I'm not too handy with mine either,' Baldur said, apparently indifferent to having his picture snapped, if he even realized that this is what she had done.

'I worked as a caretaker for several years,' he carried on, in answer to her earlier question, 'but they were getting rid of people and I was one of the first they let go. Apart from that, I've changed jobs a lot, never stuck at one thing for long. I used to work for tradesmen, mostly, working with my hands, you know the sort of thing.'

Hulda had to admit to herself that she couldn't picture Baldur in the role of murderer; he seemed the type who wouldn't hurt a fly. And while appearances could be deceptive, she reckoned she was quite a good judge of character after so many years in the police, dealing with all sorts of people, both on the wrong and the right side of the law. Her judgement wasn't infallible, though. It had let her down badly in one instance . . . And that had been her greatest mistake, changing her life for ever.

And even if she was right in her view that Baldur would be incapable of murdering a woman in cold blood, there was still an outside chance that he could be implicated in Elena's death. For all Hulda knew, he could, at some point in the past, have accepted the offer of a dodgy but well-remunerated job and fallen in with the wrong crowd as a result.

'Your brother had some papers for me,' she reminded him politely.

Baldur's face fell. Clearly, he had been hoping she would stick around a bit longer, chatting over bad coffee.

'Of course.' He got up and left the room, returning almost immediately with a brown envelope. 'Here you go. I don't know what's in it, but I hope it'll come in useful. Albert should know, as a former cop.'

Hulda resisted the temptation to correct him: Albert had never been a cop; he'd only worked for the police as a lawyer. 'Mm,' she said non-committally, then pushed back her chair and stood up, conspicuously checking her watch to hint that she had to get going.

'Did you work with him yourself?' asked Baldur, in a transparent attempt to spin out their conversation a little longer.

'Not directly, but I remember him. He was pretty well thought of,' she said, though she had no idea if this was true.

Baldur smiled: 'That's nice to hear.'

He seemed such a genuine, friendly soul. Even from this brief acquaintance, Hulda found it hard to believe he could be linked to the case, but it would be up to Dóra to settle the matter.

Hulda took her leave, forcing herself to wait until she was outside before looking in the envelope, though she was so consumed by curiosity she would have liked to tear it open then and there.

So it came as a huge disappointment to discover that the papers – a quick shuffle revealed ten pages – were all in Russian. She leafed through them several times in the hope of finding something she could understand, skimming the text on every page, but it was no good. Some were handwritten, others computer printouts, the rest clearly official documents, but she hadn't a clue what information they contained.

Taking out her phone, she considered calling a state-registered translator, but she could leave that until tomorrow. Instead, she would drive out to Njarðvík and show Dóra Baldur's mugshot; see where that got her.

No, the documents had to take priority. Hulda was on the point of ringing to book a Russian translator when her phone bleeped to indicate an incoming text. It was from Magnús. Damn, she still needed to call him back. The message read: 'Meet me at the office now!', the exclamation mark speaking volumes. Her heart skipped a beat. She'd never had much time for Magnús, especially in the present circumstances, and wasn't above bitching about him with her colleagues when she was confident that they felt the same. And she'd lost count of the thousands of times she'd cursed him under her breath for his general incompetence as a manager. But, when all was said and done, he was still her boss, and his message had the intended effect. Temporarily shelving any idea of getting the documents translated or visiting Dóra, she jumped to obey his command. She was being summoned for a reprimand, that much was clear; a completely new experience for her.

XXI

The snow had stopped after that first brief flurry, but the sky was leaden with clouds promising more to come.

Suddenly, without any warning, he made a sharp turn, leaving the road and starting out across country, making for a distant range of mountains. She flinched and braced herself, clinging to the door handle. 'Is this a road?' she asked, alarmed.

He shook his head. 'Nope,' he said, 'we're driving on the snow-crust. This is where the fun really begins.' He grinned, as if to underline that he was being humorous.

After sitting in silence for a while, she ventured to ask if there was any risk they might damage the terrain. Were they allowed to do this? Something about the untouched landscape struck a chord with her; it felt as if they were driving through an uninhabited wilderness where no human had ever set foot before; as if they had no right to be there.

'Don't be stupid,' he snapped. 'Of course it's allowed.'

She was a little taken aback by his tone, unsure how to react, but then she didn't know him very well. Was it possible that he had a darker side, lurking under that friendly exterior?

She tried to shrug off her sense of disquiet.

'Want a go?' he asked abruptly.

'What?' she asked.

'Want a go?' he repeated. 'At driving.'

'I can't. I've never driven a four-by-four, and I've never driven off-road like this, in snow this deep.'

'Don't be silly, have a go,' he said, smiling, as if it was all just friendly banter.

She shook her head doubtfully.

His response was to brake and kill the engine, out there in the middle of nowhere, the road far behind, and the mountains, their apparent goal, even further off ahead.

'This is where you take over,' he said smoothly, and, without more ado, jumped down from the car, marched round and opened the door on the passenger side. 'It's child's play. There's nothing to it. I promised you an adventure, remember?'

Nervously, she climbed down from her seat, picked her way gingerly through the deep snow to the driver's side and got behind the wheel. Luckily, the four-by-four was a manual and she was used to manuals, so she switched on the ignition, put the car carefully into first gear and set off at a crawl, slowly breaking a path through the snow.

'You can go faster than that,' he taunted, and she changed warily into second, putting her foot down a little more firmly on the accelerator.

'Over there — to your right; the going's better there,' he directed, peering at the confusing image on the satnav fixed to the inside of the windscreen. 'Now, quick! We need to avoid those tussocks of grass.'

She made a sharp right. The conditions left little leeway for mistakes and, for a moment, she was afraid she wouldn't make the bend and that they would roll. Her heart was hammering against her ribcage, but the car made it safely round.

'It's a bloody nightmare getting stuck in a patch of tussocks,' he explained, then peered at the satnav again. 'Now you're crossing a river,' he announced, and laughed.

'Crossing a river? Seriously? Is there a river underneath us?' Her heart began to pound again.

'Sure, there's water all over the place, under the ice.'

'Are you absolutely sure it's safe?'

'Well . . .' He paused for effect. 'We'll just have to hope the ice doesn't give way right now.'

She clutched the wheel involuntarily, and his mocking laughter did nothing to allay her fears.

XXII

The farmhouse was situated on a mountainside near the coast, in a sparsely populated district not far from the vast, flat sands that stretched between the Vatnajökull ice cap and the sea. From the yard where the mother stood holding her daughter by the hand, there was a breathtaking panorama of mountains, glaciers, sandy plains and sea. She had never visited the remote south-east of the country before and, while she couldn't deny the magnificence of the scenery, that wasn't why she was here. She had come to say goodbye to her daughter: to give her up for adoption, leave her behind among strangers in this isolated spot.

In spite of her valiant efforts to hold back the tears, her father had evidently sensed her reluctance. He had made a point of praising the couple's generosity and stressing how healthy it would be for the little girl to grow up in the countryside, surrounded by nature and fresh sea air. The child would be quick to adapt, he assured her: she'd already experienced one big change in her life, and, unfair though it was to expect her to go through another so soon, it would be best to get it over with. After all, what prospects did she have in town? None of them had any money to speak of and all they had to look forward to was hard grind and an unrelenting struggle to put food on the table. That sort of life was tough on kids, and his granddaughter deserved better. Hanging unspoken between father and daughter was the fact that the couple from the east had offered to compensate the family for their outlay, and that this compensation was out of all proportion to the cost they had incurred in bringing up the child. Though neither would have put it into words, they knew they were in effect selling the little girl – for a sum so considerable that it would make a real difference to their lives. Blood money, that's what it was. The girl's mother had already made up her mind not to touch a penny of it. Her father could do what he liked; use it to pay off his debts if he wanted to. But, much as she hated to acknowledge it, the truth was that she stood to gain as well, directly or indirectly, for as long as she lived with her parents.

She hung back, clutching her daughter's hand, while her father walked slowly up to the house. The owners must be aware that they had arrived: there was no one else around.

She noticed that her daughter was shivering: perhaps it was the icy wind blowing down from the mountains in spite of the beautiful weather. Or perhaps the little girl could sense that something awful, something momentous, was about to happen.

How could I have let myself be talked into this? It was all the mother could think as she watched her father walking up to the front door.

Scooping the little girl into her arms, she hugged her tight, trying to stop her shivering. It had been a long journey by plane and road to get here. A young man, presumably one of the farmhands, had collected them from the airport. He was still sitting in the car, no doubt under orders not to intrude on the delicate meeting that was about to take place.

The door opened to reveal a man in late middle age, who greeted them warmly. And now there was no turning back. Tears were pouring down the mother's cheeks. The little girl, seeing this, began to whimper as well. The two men, who were old friends, glanced at them then carried on their conversation. Mother and child were mere extras, with only a limited role in the great scheme of things. How ironic that the girl's grandmother, the driving force behind this decision, had been unable to face coming with them.

The mother felt how quickly and surely her embrace calmed the little girl and stilled her shivering. It came to her then that she felt like the girl's real mother, not just the lady behind the glass, and she hoped – maybe against hope – that the little girl felt the same about her.

There was a shout. Her father was calling them over, telling them to come inside. She balked, all her doubts rising to the surface. After taking a few halting steps towards the house, she stopped dead. The couple were both standing in the doorway now, wearing smiles intended to be kind, yet their kindness didn't strike her as genuine. It was as if they were only smiling to win her over.

And suddenly her mind was made up: she wasn't going to set foot in that house, wasn't going to leave little Hulda with them.

'I'm going home,' she announced in a clear voice that surprised her with its firmness. Her father stared at her without speaking. 'I'm going home,' she repeated, 'and Hulda's coming with me.'

He came over, put his arms around them both and said: 'Fair enough, it's your choice.'

He was smiling.

She clasped her little girl tight, vowing never to let her go again.

XXIII

Hulda had been sitting in her car outside the police station for several minutes, unable to summon up the courage to go in, dreading the coming encounter with Magnús. Not that she regretted anything. It had been the right decision to take a closer look into Elena's death and she had no intention of dropping her investigation without a fight. The visit to Áki had been necessary, though in hindsight, perhaps she should have been in less of a hurry and done a bit more intelligence gathering first. But that was the fault of the tight deadline she had set herself to solve the case.

Almost without thinking, she found that she had taken out her phone and dialled Pétur's number. He answered immediately.

'Hulda,' he said cheerfully. 'I've been waiting for you to call.' He seemed to be in a perpetual good mood, always positive and sunny tempered. Yes, she really liked him: how could she not?

'Oh?' she said, and instantly regretted this curt reply,

which had been motivated by surprise at his statement rather than any intention to be rude.

'Yes, I thought maybe we could meet up again this evening. I was going to offer to cook dinner for you at my place.'

'That would be lovely,' Hulda replied, tricked for a moment by the light evening into forgetting that it was long past suppertime. 'I mean . . . it would have been great.'

'Let's do it, anyway. I can cook for you now. I've got all the ingredients, including a very nice joint of lamb – I can stick it on the barbecue while I'm waiting.' As an afterthought, he added: 'Unless you've already eaten?'

'What? No, no, I haven't actually.' The hot dog didn't count. 'I, er, I'll look forward to it.' She realized she was short of breath, stressed about her impending conversation with Magnús, and hoped Pétur wouldn't notice and start asking awkward questions.

She acknowledged to herself that she felt a warm glow inside at the thought of visiting him. She desperately needed to talk to someone: about Elena and the case, about giving up work. And then there were those other things she needed to tell him.

'Great. Are you on your way? How long will you be?'

'I've got to drop into the office first. Won't be long.' At least, she hoped not.

The corridor leading to Magnús's office had never felt so endless. His door was open and, just as she raised her hand to tap on the glass and alert him to her presence, he glanced up. His brows were drawn together in a grave frown and she saw at once that their meeting was going to be difficult. She had an uneasy feeling that it was solely on her account that he had come in to work on this beautiful spring evening. What on earth had she done wrong? Should she have secured clearer permission to reopen the inquiry? Or had Áki complained about her? She could easily imagine a man like him having influential friends in high places.

'Sit down,' Magnús barked.

Normally, she would have been affronted by his tone, but this time she was so anxious that she meekly dropped into the seat facing him and waited. She hadn't so much as opened her mouth yet.

'Did you pay a visit to Áki Ákason earlier this evening?'

She nodded. Not much point trying to deny it.

'What in God's name were you thinking of?' Magnús's annoyance seemed to have spilled over into rage.

Hulda winced. She had been ready for a slap on the wrist, but not for him to blow his top like this.

'What do you mean? I . . . I was acting on a –'

He cut her short: 'That's right, out with it, explain yourself. I don't want to have to fire you when you're about to retire anyway.'

Hulda pulled herself together. 'I received a tip-off that he was involved in trafficking or a prostitution racket, something like that.'

'And where did this tip-off come from?'

Hulda wouldn't dream of dropping Karen in it. 'A

source: I can't reveal their name, but I . . . I've usually been able to rely on . . . him.'

Had Karen given her dud information? Had she gone round to see an honest businessman and accused him of taking part in organized crime? That would be one hell of a cock-up.

'And why, may I ask, have you taken it upon yourself to investigate a trafficking ring?' Magnús asked, in a voice dripping with contempt.

'You told me to pick a case.'

'Pick a case?' Magnús echoed, puzzled.

'Yes, to work on until I have to leave.'

'Oh, I see, but . . . I didn't for one minute think you'd take me seriously. It was just a casual suggestion. I thought you'd go home and relax, play a round of golf, or whatever it is you do for kicks.'

'I go hiking in the mountains.'

'Well, then, I thought you'd go hiking or something. What the hell do you think you're doing, investigating a case without telling me?'

'I was under the impression that I had your permission.' Her voice was steadier, her heartbeat had slowed; she was marshalling her weapons.

'And what case is that, then?'

'The Russian woman who died: the one found on Vatnsleysuströnd.'

'I see. Alexander's case, wasn't it? That was solved ages ago.'

'I'm not so sure about that. His investigation was a disgrace.'

'What are you saying?' Magnús asked sharply.

'Come on, Magnús. You know as well as I do that Alexander's methods are hit and miss, at best.' Hulda was a little surprised at her own nerve. It was something she had always wanted to say but never dared. But then, she had nothing to lose now.

Magnús didn't immediately answer, then eventually conceded: 'Maybe he's not our very best detective but . . .'

'Never mind that. You'll just have to trust me on this. I believe there's something there, something we've overlooked. If she was murdered, it's our duty to find out.'

'No . . . no . . . the case is closed,' Magnús said, but she could hear the hesitation in his voice.

'You can't just sack me. I must have some rights after all these years.'

He was silent a moment, then asked abruptly: 'So where does Áki come in?'

'There's a chance the Russian girl was brought over to work in the sex industry. I'm sorry if I was given the wrong information: I didn't mean to bother an innocent man.'

'Innocent man?' Magnús laughed, though he didn't sound in the least amused. 'He's guilty as hell. That's the whole bloody problem.'

'What do you mean?'

'He runs a major sex-trafficking outfit.'

'So it wasn't him who complained about me?'

'Are you out of your mind? God, no, we haven't heard a peep out of him. No, you've just managed to jeopardize months of hard work. We've been keeping him under surveillance and, as far as we know, he didn't have the faintest idea until this evening – all thanks to you.'

Hulda was appalled. 'You mean I –?'

'Yes, you . . . Our people were monitoring the premises and saw you go inside, but by then it was too late: the damage had been done. There's no way of knowing what he's up to now – warning his accomplices, destroying evidence. The team's holding a crisis meeting as we speak, trying to decide whether to cut their losses and arrest him now. The trouble is, they needed more time to collect evidence against him. It's a bloody mess. And you'll be blamed for that. Which means *I'll* get it in the neck.'

'I don't know what to say. I simply hadn't a clue.'

'Of course you didn't have a fucking clue! Because you didn't bother to check with anyone first. It's always the same problem with you – a total failure to collaborate.' Magnús banged his fist on the desk. 'Always the same bloody story.'

Hulda bridled at this: 'I didn't always have a choice, you know. You and your mates, you haven't exactly been eager to "collaborate" over the years. I've sometimes been forced to slog through cases alone because no one's been willing to work with me. You boys stick together and shut me out. Oh, I'm not complaining – it's too late for that and, anyway, it's not my style – but I want you to know what it's been like, before the next woman has to go through the same crap.'

Magnús seemed astonished by her reaction. 'I've treated you no differently from anyone else in this department. I don't have to sit here and listen to this.'

Hulda shrugged. 'You know better than that, Magnús. But I'm leaving, so it's not my problem any more.'

'I think this meeting has gone on long enough. The case is closed.'

This time, it was Hulda who slammed her fist on the desk. She kept taking herself by surprise, all her pent-up rage bursting forth: 'No. I need more time to finish this. Surely you owe me that much, at least?'

Magnús sat frozen at this outburst, his face expressionless.

'I need a few more days, maybe a week. I'll keep you informed so there's no danger of my treading on my colleagues' toes again. That was completely unintentional, as you know full well.'

He sat and thought about it, before grudgingly conceding: 'All right. You can have one day.'

'One day? There's no way that's enough.'

'Well, it'll bloody well have to be. I've had it up to here with you. You'll just have to get an early start. We'll make a deal: I'll leave you alone tomorrow, OK? But the day after that, you're coming in here and clearing your desk. Then you can start getting used to your retirement.'

XXIV

The light was failing.

After driving for a while, she had more or less got the hang of coping with the snow. The four-by-four answered well to the steering wheel and the hard-frozen crust bore up under their weight. The promised blizzard hadn't materialized yet, though a few flakes had begun to fall, enough to justify switching on the wipers.

He had been right after all: this was part of the package, part of the adventure she had signed up for. She regretted now that she had shrunk away from the challenge.

Once she'd had a good go, he'd taken over the wheel again and driven at a cracking pace until a mountain loomed up ahead, at which point he took his foot off the accelerator and slowed to a stop.

'This'll do. We'll leave the car here.'

Stepping out into a light mist of snow, she surveyed their surroundings. 'Are we going up there, up the mountain?' she asked doubtfully, quailing at the sight of the sheer black crags showing through the white.

He shook his head. 'No, not all the way, just into the valley over the next ridge. The going'll be a bit challenging, though.'

Darkness was closing in with frightening speed and she only hoped they would make it to their destination while it was still twilight. The night would be impenetrable here: no distant glow from a town; nothing but mountains and snow.

'Will . . . will there be any other people about?'

'Nobody else comes out here,' he said flatly.

He had begun to unload the car and their rucksacks were already lying in the snow beside the other equipment. Reaching into one of them, he pulled out a thick jumper, a traditional lopapeysa, hand-knitted from Icelandic wool, with a distinctive zig-zagging pattern in white, brown and grey around the yoke.

'Here. Put this on or you'll freeze,' he said, grinning. In the twilight, it was hard to see what sort of grin it was.

She obeyed without protest, taking off her thick down jacket. A shiver spread through her body. Probably just the cold, she told herself, but on second thoughts, maybe . . . maybe it was fear.

He handed her the rucksack and, staggering a little under the weight, she hoisted it on to her back. He helped her with the straps before fixing the ice axe to the outside.

They hadn't gone more than a few paces before she realized she'd forgotten to put on her gloves. In what seemed like moments, she had lost all sensation in her fingers and had to call him to ask for help with digging the gloves out of her pack. Once he had done this, they resumed their march, plodding onwards through the thickening snow until, finally, he halted.

'We're going to try and climb up here. Do you think you can make it?'

Ahead, she saw a steep, white slope rising up to invisible heights, the top obscured by the failing light and the snowflakes stinging her eyes.

'Do you think you can make it?' he asked again.

She nodded doubtfully and waited for him to lead the way.

'You first,' he prompted, after a short silence. She couldn't believe her ears. There was no way she was tackling this slope alone and unaided.

'Me? Why?'

'I'm not sure how firm the snow is up there. If there's an avalanche, I'll be able to dig you out.'

She stood there, rigid with fear, wondering if he was joking but afraid that he was deadly serious.

He handed her the walking poles that had been fixed to the outside of her backpack and told her to get a move on.

Since there was nothing for it, she set off, picking her way up with extreme caution. The incline wasn't too steep at first, but it increased sharply the higher she climbed. She tried to concentrate on taking one step at a time, keeping her eyes down, trying not to lose her balance. Every now and then she peered up, but the white ground and falling snow merged into one and she couldn't for the life of her see where the slope ended. It was becoming more and more difficult to lift her feet and ever trickier to find a purchase. Soon she was sliding backwards with every step, sometimes taking several attempts to gain a few centimetres in height. She tried to kick footholds in the snow using the toes of her boots, but with limited success, until in a moment of dizzying fear she felt herself losing her balance and slid halfway back down the way she had come.

XXV

A few clouds streaked the sky above the tall firs in Pétur's garden, as if painted with broad brushstrokes on the blue vault of the heavens, and the sun was descending towards its late setting. Usually, it was a time of year that filled Hulda with vitality, but not today. She was utterly drained of energy following her meeting with Magnús, too weary to put any more work into the investigation: Elena would have to wait until morning.

Pétur opened the door before she could knock, having no doubt been watching out for her from the kitchen window. She tried not to let her exhaustion show.

'Hulda! Come in.' His manner was as warm as ever, like a doctor talking to his favourite patient. He led the way into the sitting room that doubled as a dining room, where the table was already laid, with the most succulent-looking joint of lamb, obviously hot off the barbecue, as the *pièce de résistance*. It smelled so delicious that Hulda belatedly realized she was famished. Pétur had opened a bottle of red wine, too, as she'd hoped he would. Just as well she'd taken the precaution of dropping her car off at home and ringing for a taxi.

'This looks good,' she said.

He offered her a chair and she sank into it gratefully, feeling the fatigue flowing out of her limbs. Pétur vanished into the kitchen. Sitting there felt a little strange, as if she didn't belong, as if she were a gatecrasher. Yet, another part of her felt as if she had come home. Perhaps it was the garden that she could see from the living-room windows, reminding her a little of her old garden on Álftanes.

Pétur's place was warm but, more than that, it had a cosy, homely air. Yes, she could easily picture herself living here, enjoying Pétur's company, cooking dinner with him, drinking wine into the night . . .

'Long day?' Pétur asked, coming back in with a bowl of vegetables. 'Mine was pretty quiet. You'll appreciate that once you've retired – a fit woman like you, with outside interests.' He smiled.

'I suppose so,' Hulda replied ruefully. 'Yes, you could say I've had a rather . . . trying day.'

Pétur sat down. 'Help yourself while it's hot. It's usually very good barbecued this way. Makes a nice change to have someone else to cook for.'

'Thanks.' She took a mouthful. The flavour was exceptional: Pétur was clearly an excellent cook. That was a definite plus.

'What's happened?' he asked.

'What?'

'Today. Something's happened, I can tell.'

Hulda considered how much to share with him. Discussing the case wasn't a problem, since she had complete faith in Pétur's discretion, but she felt reluctant to describe her meeting with Magnús. This was partly out of shame at her blunder, however well intentioned it had been.

After a silence that lasted a minute or two yet somehow never became uncomfortable, she surprised herself by saying: 'I had a meeting with my boss. He wants me to drop the investigation.'

'Immediately?'

'Yes.'

'Why? Are you going to?'

'I interviewed a man I shouldn't have. It's a long story but, basically, my inquiry overlapped with another investigation. I hadn't a clue it was going on, though I have to admit that was partly my fault for not keeping my boss in the loop. He had no idea what I was up to.' She heaved a sigh. 'The detective who originally handled the case is furious with me as well. To be honest, I'm in a bit of a mess.'

'It's bound to sort itself out. I'm sure of that.' As usual, Pétur seemed unperturbed. 'And if I know you, you won't give up without a fight.'

Hulda laughed. 'No, I managed to squeeze one more day out of him. My last day.'

'Then you'd better make good use of it.'

'You can say that again.' She raised her glass and took the first sip. 'In other words, I'd better go easy on this superb wine.'

'And once tomorrow's over, you'll be free. Congratulations!'

'You certainly know how to look on the bright side.'

'Shouldn't we celebrate your retirement?'

'If you like,' Hulda said, her voice mellow. 'This is quite a celebration we're having already. It's absolutely delicious.'

'We could climb Esja,' Pétur suggested. 'What do you say to that? I've lost track of how many times I've been up there, but I never get tired of it. Not everyone's lucky enough to have a mountain like that in their backyard. And the view of the city on a clear day . . .'

'You don't have to convince me – I'm in,' Hulda replied, and for the first time in ages she found herself genuinely looking forward to something. Just for a moment, she toyed with the idea of abandoning Elena and putting herself first, giving in to Magnús's wish for her to retire with immediate effect. She was on the point of suggesting they climb Esja tomorrow instead.

The words teetered on the tip of her tongue.

But when she did speak it was to say: 'Right, the day after tomorrow it is. I'll need one more day for the inquiry.' And instantly she experienced a powerful, unsettling premonition that this had been the wrong decision.

For the second evening in a row, they overdid the red wine. Hulda was dreading the morning, worrying that she would oversleep again and be too hung-over to achieve anything useful. But Pétur seemed to like having her there, and she had to admit that she was enjoying his company. It was well past midnight; the hours had passed in a blur, conversation seemed to come so easily to them.

Reluctant to put an end to a lovely evening, Hulda sat tight on his leather sofa.

They were sitting side by side now, still a discreet distance apart. Pétur was obviously taking care not to get too close: he knew what he was doing.

'You told me yesterday that you'd never met your father,' he remarked.

Hulda nodded.

'Did your mother ever marry? Or did she bring you up on her own?'

'No, she never married. We lived with my grandparents,' Hulda said. 'My grandfather and I were great friends – he was the person I was closest to. I think we must have been very alike in some ways. I suppose he was like a bridge to that side of my family. My mother and I were never that close, but thanks to Granddad I felt I belonged, if you know what I mean. I never met my relatives on my father's side. Without Granddad, I don't think my childhood would have been a very happy one.'

Pétur nodded and she sensed that he understood.

'I'd like to have met my father,' she went on, in a low, disconsolate voice, feeling weepy all of a sudden. That was the wine: she knew she was tipsy but was enjoying it too much to stop drinking.

'What was it like,' Pétur began, considerately changing the subject, though without straying too far from what they had been discussing, 'growing up with a single mother in those days? I know it's taken for granted now, but I remember how people used to talk about one of my schoolfriends who didn't have a father – I mean, no one knew who his father was.'

'It was tough,' Hulda acknowledged, reaching out for the bottle and refilling their empty glasses. 'Very tough. She was forever changing jobs, from what I remember. It was unusual at the time for a woman to be a breadwinner, as you know, and she couldn't always work as much as she wanted to because of me. It was a real struggle. We were quite hard up – I don't think it's any exaggeration to say that. The only reason we had a roof over our heads was because we were lucky enough to live with my grandparents. We always had food on the table but there was no money to spare for anything else; none of us could afford any luxuries. Growing up, I found that hard, as I'm sure you can imagine.'

'Well, to be honest, I can't really imagine what that's like,' Pétur said slowly. 'My father was a doctor like me, so we were always well off. Luckily. The worst thing about poverty is the effect it has on the children.'

'Actually . . .' Hulda broke off, feeling a bit fuddled by the wine and wondering about the wisdom of what she had been about to say. How much ought she to tell this man? Could she trust him? Then again, maybe it would be good, healthy even, to open up about the past once in a while. She'd been bottling things up for far too long: maybe this was the chance she'd been waiting for. She had never been able to discuss personal matters at the office. None of her younger colleagues was remotely interested in hearing about the ups and downs in the life of a sixty-four-year-old woman. What's more, she could count her friends, her *real* friends, on the fingers of one hand, on a good day. She decided to risk it: 'Actually, things could have turned out very differently.'

'Oh?' said Pétur. His answer came so promptly, with no sign of slurring, that Hulda wondered hazily if she had knocked back more of the wine than him.

'My mother put me in an institution when I was a baby – a home for infants, almost like an orphanage. I heard the story from Granddad; my mother never breathed a word about it to me. It was considered the right and proper thing for unmarried mothers to do in those days. From hints Granddad dropped, I think he and Grandma must have pressurized her into it and that, later, he came to regret it. He said I was taken away from my mother shortly after I was born. Do you remember those homes?'

'Not personally, though of course I've heard about them.'

'Apparently, my mother visited regularly, which is only natural, I suppose. Granddad said he was proud of her. As soon as she'd managed to save up enough money, she went and claimed me. She had every right to, though I think the babies in those institutions were usually fostered or adopted.'

'Were you there long?' asked Pétur.

'Nearly two years. And as if that wasn't bad enough, in all that time my mother was never once allowed to touch me or hold me. I gather parents were only allowed to see their babies through a glass partition. The staff thought that if the parents got to cuddle them, it would be too hard on the children when they left.'

'I don't suppose you remember . . . ?' Pétur left the question hanging.

'No, I don't have any memory of that time,' said Hulda. 'I was far too young. But I did once visit the building where the home used to be. This was donkey's years ago. Walking through the door was such a weird feeling. I had this overwhelming sensation of déjà vu. The glass partition had gone, but I've seen pictures of it. And as I was walking along the corridor I instinctively stopped dead by one closed door and asked the woman showing me round whether the children used to sleep in there. She nodded and said I was quite right, and the moment she opened the door it hit me. I knew, I just knew, that I'd slept in that room. You don't have to believe me, but it was a peculiar experience.'

'I believe you,' said Pétur. As ever, he answered without hesitation and said exactly the right thing.

'I do have one genuine memory from early childhood,' Hulda continued. 'There were plans to have me fostered – this was after my mother had taken me back and we were living with my grandparents. A couple were interested in adopting me. Again, I heard this from Granddad, not from my mother, though I have no reason to doubt what he said, and this time I actually remember something about it. I remember the flight – it must have been to the east. That would fit in with the location because the couple lived between the glacial sands in the Skaftafell district and it used to be quite a palaver to get there in those days. I've never forgotten that journey, though I was only a toddler at the time. We never used to leave

Reykjavík, so I suppose I've retained memories from the trip because it was so unusual.'

'Tell me . . .' Pétur hesitated, as if unsure whether to continue. 'Perhaps it's an inappropriate question . . .'

'Fire away,' said Hulda, and immediately regretted it.

'Well . . . If you could choose now, in retrospect, would you have wanted to grow up with your mother?'

The question threw Hulda, perhaps precisely because she had often, almost unconsciously, wondered the same thing, without coming to any definite conclusion. Had her childhood been happy? Not really; perhaps not at all. But there was no way of knowing if the grass would have been greener if she had been brought up by strangers. Did money matter? Had the poverty of her upbringing, the endless striving to make ends meet, had a lasting effect on her?

She cast her mind back to her early years, trying to recall some happy memories. There was the one where she was sitting in her bedroom listening to a story; she couldn't remember what the story was about, but the memory was vivid and warm. The person sitting next to her then had been her granddad, not her mother. She also recalled a trip, when she was maybe eight or nine, to the corner shop, which had been closed for many years now. She had gone there to spend her own money, a small fortune which she had saved up by working for her granddad in the summer, helping him with bits of DIY around the small flat. Everything was linked to her granddad, not her mother, and yet her mother had always been so kind to her.

She took her time answering. 'I have to admit, between you and me, and I'm holding the wine to blame if I regret this conversation later, that I could have had a happier childhood, though whether being fostered would have solved the problem is impossible to say. What I do believe, what I'm sure of, is that my life would have been better if I'd been allowed to stay with my mother from the beginning. I know children aren't supposed to remember anything about their first few years, but remembering is one thing, sensing is another. I believe I picked up on the insecurity and that it's affected me all my life. I also believe that my poor mother felt guilty from the moment she handed me over to her dying day. And guilt can be a heavy burden.'

'I'm sorry, Hulda, I didn't mean to be . . . intrusive.'

'It doesn't matter. I'm through being over-sensitive about the past. What's done is done. No point crying over spilt milk, and all that. Though, inevitably, you do regret some things: they're always lying in wait to ambush you in your dreams.' Hulda allowed a silence to fall, her gaze wandering around the handsome living room, reflecting not for the first time that Pétur had never known what it was like to go without.

He opened his mouth to speak but she got in first: 'You're always asking about me.' She smiled to show that this wasn't intended as a criticism. 'Let's talk about you now. Did you and your wife build this house?'

'Yes, we did, as a matter of fact. It's been a wonderful place to live. A good location, of course, a nice area. We came very close to selling it at one time, but I'm extremely glad we didn't. I'm very attached to it. It holds so many memories – both good and bad, of course – and I have every intention of staying put, although it's far too big.' After a beat, he added: 'Too big for one person, that is.'

'Why?'

'I'm sorry?'

'Why did you come close to selling it?' Her detective instincts alerted, she had pounced unerringly on that hint of evasiveness.

Pétur didn't answer straight away. He got up and fetched another bottle, then settled on the sofa again, still at a polite distance.

'It looked as if we were heading for a divorce at one point, about fifteen years ago.' Hulda could tell that it was an effort for him to talk about this.

She waited without speaking.

After a lengthy pause and another sip of wine, Pétur elaborated: 'She had an affair. It had been going on for several years without my having a clue. When I discovered by accident, she moved out. I sued for divorce, and it had almost gone through when she came round to see me and begged for a second chance.'

'Did you find it easy to forgive her?'

'Yes, I did, actually. Perhaps because it was her and I'd been in love with her all those years. That never changed. But I think it's just my nature. I've always been quick to forgive. Don't know why.'

On hearing this, Hulda reflected that maybe they weren't as well suited as she'd thought. Because she was certainly not quick to forgive.

'You mentioned you used to live out on Álftanes?' he asked, changing the subject. 'Did you have a house there?'

'Yes, it was . . .' She paused to choose her words carefully. 'It was a gorgeous spot, right by the sea. I still miss the sound of the waves. How about you? Have you ever lived by the sea?'

'At one time. My father was a doctor out east, but I'm a city boy, really. Grew up to the roar of traffic rather than surf. Did you sell up when your husband died?'

'Yes, I couldn't afford the upkeep.'

'You said he died quite young, didn't you?'

'He was fifty-two.'

'Awful, just awful.'

Hulda nodded.

Despite the gloomy subjects they were discussing, the sitting room seemed like a haven of tranquillity. Outside, the night was as dim as it ever got in May. But at that moment her phone rang, shattering the peace with its loud, intrusive racket. With an apologetic glance at Pétur, Hulda scrabbled in the depths of her bag. It came as a surprise, to put it mildly, when she saw who was calling, especially since it was past midnight. It was the nurse who had knocked down the paedophile; the woman Hulda had given such a big break to by pretending that her confession had never taken place. She had hoped never to hear another word about the incident.

Hulda cut off the call without answering it. 'Sorry, never a moment's peace.'

'You're telling me.' Pétur smiled.

Hulda put the phone on the table beside the new bottle

of red. Clearly, they weren't finished yet; there was plenty of wine left.

Her phone rang again.

'Damn it,' Hulda muttered, louder than she'd intended.

'Go ahead and answer,' Pétur said kindly. 'It doesn't bother me.'

But Hulda had absolutely no desire to speak to the wretched woman, who was probably still in a state about the crime she had committed and desperate to relieve her conscience by unburdening to the only other person who knew the truth. Hulda had no intention of acting as her confessor, especially not now. She was enjoying Pétur's company and there was no reason to go and ruin the atmosphere.

'No, it's nothing urgent. In fact, I can't understand why she's ringing this late. So inconsiderate.' Hulda cut the call again, and this time switched her phone off. 'There, perhaps we'll be left in peace now.'

'More wine?' Pétur asked, eyeing her half-empty glass.

'I don't mind if I do, thanks. It had better be my last, though. I've got to work tomorrow, remember.'

Pétur filled her glass. There followed rather a long silence. Hulda had nothing to say; she was too tired, and the alcohol didn't help.

'Was it a deliberate decision on your part not to have any children?' Pétur asked, a little unexpectedly. Perhaps it was a natural continuation of the conversation about Hulda's husband.

The question caught her unprepared, though she should have known that, sooner or later, she would have to tell Pétur; at least she would if their relationship continued along this path.

She took a while to work out how to answer and Pétur waited with characteristic patience. He didn't seem to let much bother him.

'We had a daughter,' she said at last, plumping for the simple answer.

'I'm sorry, I thought . . .' Pétur seemed surprised and a little confused. 'I thought you said . . . I was under the impression that you and your husband didn't have any children.'

'That's because I deliberately avoided the subject. You'll have to forgive me – I still find it hard to talk about.' Hearing her voice breaking, Hulda fought to stop her face from crumpling. 'She died.'

'I don't know what to say,' Pétur replied hesitantly. 'I'm terribly sorry to hear that.'

'She killed herself.'

Hulda could feel the tears sliding down her cheeks. It was true that she wasn't used to talking about this. Although she thought about her daughter every day, she hardly ever spoke of her.

Pétur didn't say a word.

'She was so young, only just turned thirteen. We didn't try for any more children after that. Jón was fifty, I was ten years younger.'

'God . . . You've really been through the wringer, Hulda.'

'I can't talk about it, sorry. Anyway, that's what happened. Then Jón died and I've been alone ever since.'

'That could be about to change,' Pétur said.

Hulda tried to smile but felt suddenly ambushed by tiredness. She'd had enough; she needed to go home.

Pétur seemed intuitively to know how she was feeling. 'Should we call it a night?'

Hulda shrugged. 'Yes, maybe. I had a very nice time, Pétur.'

'Shall we do it again tomorrow evening?'

'Yes,' she said, without a moment's hesitation. 'That would be lovely.'

'Perhaps we could go out for a meal somewhere? Celebrate your retirement. I'll buy you dinner at Hótel Holt. How does that sound?'

This was generous indeed. 'Gosh, yes, that would be wonderful. I haven't been there for ages. It must be more than twenty or thirty years.' The restaurant at Hótel Holt was one of the swishest establishments in Reykjavík, and Hulda did in fact remember her last visit there very well. It had been an anniversary dinner, with her husband and daughter, a happy occasion, expensive but memorable.

'I can't force my cooking on you every night. So that's settled then.'

Hulda stood up and Pétur followed suit, giving her a quick kiss on the cheek.

'The lamb was excellent,' she said. 'I wish I could barbecue meat like that.'

As they went into the hall Pétur asked abruptly: 'What was she called?'

Hulda was taken aback. Although she knew what he was asking, she pretended she didn't, to win time. 'Sorry?'

'Your daughter, what was she called?' His voice was kind, his interest genuine.

Hulda realized all of a sudden that it was years since she had last spoken her daughter's name aloud and felt ashamed of herself.

'Dimma. Her name was Dimma. Unusual, I know.' It meant 'darkness'.

The Last Day

I

Hulda rolled over in bed, unwilling to get up. Burying her head in her pillow, she tried to drift off again, but the damage was done: it was too late to try to get back to sleep now. In the old days, she had been able to enjoy a proper lie-in but, with age, this ability had become ever more elusive.

Nevertheless, when she looked at her alarm clock, she discovered to her chagrin that she had slept as late as the day before; too late, in other words.

She needed to use every minute of the day if she was going to tie up the loose ends of her investigation but, as soon as she sat up, she was hit by a splitting headache. Wonderful though the evening with Pétur had been, she shouldn't have drunk so much; she was out of practice. Normally, she had only the odd glass of wine with meals. Still, she would just have to ignore her hangover and focus on the case, though her interest in it was fast waning. Apart from a sense of duty towards the dead Russian girl, the only thing motivating her now was pure obstinacy. She simply couldn't bear to let Magnús win. Having badgered him into granting her another twenty-four hours for the inquiry, she had to give it her best shot before turning in her report this evening and saying goodbye to the police for good.

It struck her that what she was really looking forward to was her next date with Pétur. She was counting down the hours until this evening's dinner at Hótel Holt.

II

She tried to rise to her feet on the slippery snow, but that was easier said than done with the destabilizing weight of the rucksack on her back.

'Come down,' he called.

Obeying, she scrambled the rest of the way down and thanked her lucky stars when she made it safely to the bottom.

'Give me the poles,' he said. 'We'll put on the crampons and you can use your ice axe.'

Better equipped this time, she tackled the slope again, her heart in her mouth.

It was still an arduous climb but now, thanks to the crampons on her boots, she was able to get a better purchase on the snow. Inch by inch, she worked her way upwards, praying that she wouldn't lose her footing again; keeping her gaze fixed on the ground in front of her, terrified of toppling over backwards at the steepest point. One laborious step at a time, until, noticing that her progress was becoming less of an effort, she realized she was past the worst and the way ahead seemed to be getting easier. Her knees buckling with relief, she sank down on to the snow to wait, feeling mentally and physically drained. The slope was so steep that she couldn't see if he'd even started up it, let alone how far he had climbed, but she was afraid to call out to him, mindful of what he had said — half jokingly, it had seemed — about the danger of an avalanche. Why on earth had she let him talk her into this madness?

III

It was long past breakfast time and, anyway, Hulda couldn't stomach the thought of eating. Deciding to take a quick breather instead, she walked round the corner to the local supermarket. The weather was gloomier than it had been yesterday, the sky obscured by a thick layer of grey cloud, and the wind was unseasonably blustery. Could spring really have come and gone in a single day?

The weather had a dampening effect on Hulda's mood. As a rule she didn't let the unpredictable Icelandic climate get to her, but she found herself wishing that today of all days, the last day of her old life, could have got off to a more promising start.

All night long, she had been haunted by dreams of Dimma, yet in spite of this she had slept well for once. Though the dreams had been shot through with sadness, at least she had been spared the recurrent nightmare that had plagued her for years. Maybe it was a coincidence, but she suspected that talking about Dimma had been beneficial, especially to a good listener like Pétur. Perhaps one day she would feel able to open up to him about her daughter, tell him stories about her, tell him what a dear, sweet girl she had been.

Hulda roamed aimlessly up and down the aisles of the supermarket, seeing nothing to tempt her, before eventually emerging with the only items that had caught her eye: a bottle of Coke and a packet of Prins Póló chocolate wafers. Prins Póló – that took her back, reminding her of the days when Iceland used to barter with Eastern Europe, Polish chocolate in exchange for Icelandic fish. How the world had changed.

Once she had pulled herself together, the first task of the day would be to drive out to the Reykjanes peninsula and try to kill two birds – more, if possible – with one stone. She needed to talk to the Syrian girl, if it wasn't too late. Since the girl had been arrested yesterday, Hulda assumed she was being detained in the police cells at the airport, though it was equally possible that she had already been deported, sent home on one of the morning flights, which would mean Hulda had missed her chance to question her. For Christ's sake, why hadn't she made arrangements to interview her, or at the very least set an alarm this morning? She was really getting careless in the face of her imminent retirement.

She would have to stop off at the hostel in Njardvík as well, to show Dóra the photo she had sneaked of Baldur Albertsson. If Dóra wasn't there, she could always email her the picture, but she would rather witness her reaction first hand. It might be a shot in the dark but, at this stage, Hulda felt she had to keep all avenues open.

It occurred to her that it would also be worth taking this opportunity to examine the cove where Elena had died or, rather, where her body had been found. There was always a possibility that she had breathed her last somewhere else.

Hulda was behind the wheel and heading out of town before it dawned on her that she probably wasn't in a fit state to drive, with all the alcohol that must still be sloshing around in her veins. It was years since she had last found herself in this position. At the next junction, she did a U-turn and went home to call a taxi.

It was a relief to be able to slump in the back seat and relax for once, while somebody else took care of the driving, especially since the taxi was a new, luxury vehicle that purred along the Reykjanes dual carriageway with a smoothness and speed a world away from her old rust bucket.

The black lava-fields unfolded before her eyes, seeming almost to flow past the car windows, majestic in their stark simplicity, yet monotonous as an endlessly repeated refrain. She remembered reading about how they had formed, recalling that some of the lava dated from before Iceland was settled in the 800s, some of it had been produced by later eruptions. Above the flat terrain, the clouds grew heavier and blacker the further they travelled from Reykjavík, until the odd drop of rain began to spatter the windscreen.

The combination of lava and rain had a calming effect on Hulda and she let her eyelids droop, not to doze but to gather herself to face the day's demands. A series of images played through her mind, but Elena no longer occupied the foreground, having retreated behind the sharpening figures of Dimma and, now, Pétur.

She found herself dwelling more on Pétur than she'd expected, as if suddenly accepting the inevitable. Yes, age had crept up on her, taking her cruelly by surprise, but the changes it brought could be positive, too. Perhaps, after all, she deserved to be contented; to stay up late on a weekday evening, knocking back wine with a handsome doctor, without a bad conscience. Deserved a chance to forget the nightmare, once in a while. Deserved not to have to take orders from a useless boss who should never have been promoted above her.

Lost in these thoughts, she nodded off in spite of herself and slept until the driver woke her by announcing that they were nearing their destination. It took her a moment or two to work out where she was: Keflavík police station.

Falling asleep in the middle of the day was quite out of character, to say nothing of falling asleep in a taxi. There must be something in the air; everything seemed out of joint today. Hulda had a foreboding that something was about to happen, she just didn't know what.

IV

Darkness had fallen in earnest now. After he had joined her at the top of the slope, they had walked over level ground for a while before pausing briefly to fix torches to their heads. Now, she could see clearly where she was placing her feet, but all else beyond the narrow cone of light was shrouded in darkness. When she asked if they were anywhere near the place where they were to spend the night, he shook his head. 'Still a way to go,' he said.

The snow was so perfect, glittering in the light of her head torch, that it seemed like sacrilege to tread on it and break the pristine crust. Never before had she experienced such an intense connection to nature. The icy fetters seemed to cast a mysterious enchantment over their surroundings. Focusing on the elemental beauty, she did her best to forget her reservations about the trip.

Before long, the hard, icy surface gave way to deeper, softer going. Stopping for a moment, she switched off her head torch and waited for her eyes to adjust to the dark. The faint outlines of snowy knolls and mounds could be glimpsed all around them, and it came home to her more starkly than ever that without her guide she would be utterly lost; she hadn't a clue how to find the hut they were making for or retrace their steps to the car. Without him, she would almost certainly die of exposure out here.

She shuddered at the thought.

Switching on her torch again, she put her head down and set off doggedly in his wake. A gap had opened up between them and, picking up her pace, she tried to close it. She became reckless in her haste and, next thing she knew, the ground was giving way beneath her feet. Feeling herself sinking into soft snow, she started panicking that she had fallen into a hole and would never be able to get out. It turned out not to be as deep as she'd feared, but extricating herself from the clutches of the drift proved impossible, especially when weighed down by the backpack. She called out, first in a wavering voice, then louder, until he heard and, turning back, came to her rescue and heaved her out. On she went, trailing in his wake, hearing now and then the sound of water trickling under the snow, its gurgling providing a comfortingly familiar note amidst the inhuman silence of the mountains.

Abruptly, he halted, head turning this way and that, as if working out the lie of the land. She could just distinguish the dark shape of a mountain in the distance, its gully-scored slopes blurred by a layer of white.

She listened out for the river, but its gurgling had fallen quiet. Now, there was nothing but silence.

V

'Looks like you're in luck,' said the duty sergeant, who had introduced himself as Ólíver. He was tall, without an ounce of spare flesh on his lanky frame. 'Very lucky. Because that Syrian girl's still here. We were going to put her on a plane this morning, but her lawyer kicked up a stink. You know what it's like.'

'Her lawyer's not Albert Albertsson, by any chance?' Hulda asked.

'Albert? No, don't know him. The lawyer handling the Syrian's case is a woman.'

'What's her name?'

'I can't remember what any of these lawyers are called.'

'No, I meant the asylum-seeker.'

'Hmm.' Ólíver frowned. 'What was it again? … Amena, I think. Yes, Amena.'

'Why are you deporting her?'

'Some official's made a decision. Nothing to do with me. I'm just responsible for seeing her on to the plane.'

'Could I speak to her?'

Ólíver shrugged. 'Don't see why not. Though I don't know if she'll agree to meet you. I can't promise anything. Unsurprisingly, the Icelandic police aren't her favourite people right now. Why do you want to speak to her?'

He must have been thirty years younger than Hulda, but neither by his voice nor his manner did he display the slightest deference to her seniority. It was often like that these days and it never failed to rile her, the way the younger generation were taking over, rendering her redundant, as if her experience no longer counted for anything.

Hulda sighed impatiently. 'It's in connection with a case I'm investigating – an asylum-seeker found dead on the coast near here.'

Ólíver nodded. 'Yes, at Flekkuvík. I remember. Me and my partner were called to the scene when the body was found. A foreign girl, wasn't it? Couldn't handle the waiting.'

'She was Russian.'

'Yeah, that was it.'

'What do you remember about the scene?' Hulda asked.

Ólíver frowned: 'Nothing in particular. It was just another suicide, you know. She was lying there in the shallow water, obviously dead. There was nothing we could do. Why are you looking into this?'

She resisted the urge to tell him to mind his own business. 'New information. I'm not at liberty to go into details.' Leaning towards him, she whispered confidentially: 'The whole thing's a bit delicate.'

He merely shrugged again. His interest in the case clearly didn't go very deep and Hulda also got the distinct impression that he had little faith in the ability of an old bag like her to handle a police inquiry.

'All right, I'll let you speak to her, since you insist,' he said, as if addressing a naughty child.

Hulda had to bite back an angry retort.

'But both our interview rooms are in use,' he continued. 'Would you mind talking to her in her cell?'

That brought Hulda up short. She was on the point of thanking him politely and walking out, abandoning this line of investigation, when she thought better of it. 'Yes, all right, I suppose that'll do.' Might as well try to achieve something worthwhile during her last few hours in the police.

'Be right back.'

He disappeared, returning almost immediately.

'Come with me.'

He led her to a cell, opened the door then locked it again behind her. A shudder ran through Hulda as she was shut in. Whenever she'd committed some misdemeanour as a child, her grandmother used to send her to the store cupboard to reflect on her sins. The cupboard had been dark and poky and, to make matters worse, her grandmother had always locked the door. Neither Hulda's mother nor her grandfather had dared to stand up for her over the business of the naughty cupboard. Perhaps they'd thought it wasn't so bad, but for Hulda it had been a torment which left her with a lifelong phobia of being confined in narrow, enclosed spaces. In an effort to distract herself now, she cast around for something positive to focus on: the upcoming evening with Pétur, that would do. She told herself she had to be strong, for her own and Elena's sake.

The Syrian girl was a thin, wan figure, hunched in misery.

'Hello, my name's Hulda.' The girl didn't react, though Hulda had spoken in English. She was sitting on a bed that was bolted to the wall. There was no chair in the cell and, guessing that it would be unwise to sit down next to her at this stage, Hulda stayed by the door, respecting her personal space.

'Hulda,' she repeated, slowly and clearly. 'Your name's Amena, isn't it?'

The girl glanced up, meeting Hulda's eyes for an instant, before lowering her gaze to the floor again, her arms folded protectively across her chest. She was so young, not yet thirty, perhaps closer to twenty-five, and her manner was anxious, even fearful.

Hulda continued: 'I'm from the police.'

Just when she had begun to wonder if Óliver had misinformed her about the young woman's knowledge of English, Amena answered gruffly: 'I know.'

'I need to talk to you, just to ask a few questions.'

'No.'

'Why not?'

'You want to send me out of country.'

'That's nothing to do with me,' Hulda assured her, keeping her voice slow and gentle. 'I'm investigating a case and I think maybe you can help me.'

'You trick me. You want to send me home.' Amena glared at Hulda, visibly seething with impotent rage.

'No, this has nothing to do with you,' Hulda reassured her. 'It's about a Russian girl who died. Her name was Elena.'

At this, Amena became suddenly animated. 'Elena?' she said, then added with vehemence: '*I knew it*. Finally.'

'What do you mean?'

'When she die, there is something strange. I tell police officer.'

'The police officer? Was it a man? Was his name Alexander?'

'A man, yes. He don't care,' Amena said. Although her English was halting, she was perfectly capable of getting her message across.

Yet again, Hulda mentally cursed Alexander for his incompetence and prejudice. What else had he 'forgotten' to write in his report? The case had supposedly been solved, yet she felt she was fumbling her way in the dark.

'Why did you think there was something strange about her death?'

'She get permission to stay. Stay in Iceland. She get a *yes*.' The Syrian girl was emphatic.

Hulda nodded to show she understood.

The girl carried on: 'Nobody who get a yes do this. Jump in the sea. She was very happy, sit downstairs, in reception, talk all evening on the phone. Very happy. We were all very happy. She was a good girl. Warm heart. Honest. Have a difficult life in Russia. But then . . . next day she is dead. Just dead.'

Hulda nodded, while taking the description with a pinch of salt, suspecting that this rosy view of Elena might be coloured to some extent by their friendship, and by the Syrian girl's own feelings about what it must be like to be granted asylum.

The enclosed space was beginning to get to Hulda, affecting her ability to concentrate. She had broken out in a sweat, her hands were slippery and her heart was beating unnaturally fast. She had to wrap up this conversation quickly and get out of here. 'Is it possible that she was brought to Iceland to work as a prostitute?' she asked.

The question seemed to take Amena completely by surprise. 'What? Prostitute? Elena? No. No, no, no. Not possible.' She seemed to be groping for words, for a way to refute the tiny seed of doubt that Hulda's question had sown in her mind. 'No, no, I am sure. Elena was not prostitute.'

'A man was seen picking her up in his car. He was short and fat, and drove a four-by-four – a big car. I thought maybe he was a client . . .'

'No, no. Perhaps her lawyer. He drive a big car.' Amena thought for a moment then qualified this: 'But he is not fat. I don't remember name. He is not my lawyer; my lawyer is a woman.'

'Do you have any idea who the man in the big car could have been? Could he have been someone Elena knew?'

Amena shook her head. 'No, I don't think so.'

Hulda decided to bring their conversation to an end. Her claustrophobia was so bad now that she was drenched in sweat and mentally exhausted. But before she could say another word, Amena forestalled her: 'Listen, you must help me. I help you. I cannot go home. I cannot!' The raw desperation in her voice elicited an instinctive rush of pity in Hulda.

'Well, I don't suppose . . . but I'll mention it to the police officer on duty. OK?'

'Ask him to help me. Tell him I help you. Please.'

Hulda nodded again, then, changing the subject, asked: 'Do you have any idea what really happened to Elena? Did anyone have a reason to murder her and, if so, who?'

'No,' Amena replied instantly. 'No idea. She only know this lawyer. She have no enemies. Very good girl.'

'I see. Well, thanks for talking to me. I hope things work out for you. It was good to meet someone who knew Elena. What happened to her was very sad. Were you close friends? Best friends?'

'Best friends?' Amena shook her head. 'No, but we were good friends. Her best friend was Katja.'

'Katja?'

'Yes, also Russian.'

'Russian?' Hulda was so startled that she momentarily forgot her feeling of suffocation. 'Were there two Russian girls?'

'Yes. They come here together. Katja and Elena.'

Hell, Hulda thought: Katja had probably left the country months ago, which was frustrating, as Hulda would definitely have liked to talk to her. She needed to get closer to the victim, get a better sense of what had been going through her mind, who she associated with, whether she was afraid of someone, and whether she had really been trafficked to work in the sex industry.

'Do you know where Katja is?' she asked, assuming the answer would be no. 'Was she granted a residence permit, too?'

'I don't know. Nobody know.'

'What do you mean?' Hulda felt her heart beating faster, though with excitement now, rather than panic.

'She disappear.'

'She disappeared? How do you mean?'

'Yes, disappear. Or run away. She is hiding, maybe. Or leave country. I don't know.'

'When did this happen?'

The girl wrinkled her brow. 'Before Elena die. Some weeks before. Maybe one month. I am not sure.'

'Weren't you worried? How did the police react?'

'Yes . . . yes, sure. But she just run away. I should have done same . . . And nobody has found her, I think.'

'What about Elena, how did she take the news? You say they were best friends?'

'Well . . . At first she is angry. She think Katja is stupid. Think they both get permission to stay. But then . . .' Amena's face grew grave. 'Then she is worried. Very worried.'

'Was there any explanation for her disappearance?' asked Hulda, not really expecting an answer.

Amena shook her head. 'She just go, she don't want to be told to leave country. People here are . . .' She searched for the word. 'Desperate. Yes, we are all desperate.'

'What was Katja like?'

'Nice. Friendly. Very beautiful.'

'Is it possible that it was her, not Elena, who was working as a prostitute?'

'No. No, I don't believe it.'

'I see.' Hulda had been completely absorbed in the interview, but now the feeling of claustrophobia gripped her with renewed force.

Thanking Amena profusely for her help, she rapped on the door and waited, twitching with nerves, for Óliver to open it and let her out.

'You remember,' Amena said, breaking the silence. 'You will help me.'

Hulda nodded: 'I'll do my best.'

At that moment, the door opened.

'Get what you wanted?' Óliver asked, without any real interest.

'You and I need to talk. Now,' Hulda snapped, her tone that of a senior officer addressing an underling.

She stole a single backward glance before Óliver locked the cell again, and saw the Syrian girl framed for an instant by the doorway, her face the picture of despair.

VI

The river had emerged on to the surface now and they were walking along its banks in the middle of a narrow valley surrounded by mountains.

'Look,' he said suddenly, gesturing into the darkness. 'There's the hut.'

She strained her eyes in the direction he was pointing, peering through the light haze of snow, but only when they drew closer was she able to make out a tiny black dot that gradually began to take shape against the backdrop of white, revealing itself as a pitched roof on top of dark wooden walls; a tiny hut, far from civilization.

When they reached it, they found the windows and door covered in snow. He scraped the drift away from the door, but it turned out to be frozen shut and opened only after a protracted struggle. Once inside, she took off her rucksack, relieved to be free of its dragging weight. It was pitch dark, but the beams from their head torches illuminated the interior wherever they fell, revealing bunks with sleeping places for four people, maybe more. She sank down on one of the thin mattresses to catch her breath.

The hut was primitive in the extreme. It contained nothing but a small table, a few chairs and the bunks. The idea was presumably to provide basic shelter for travellers – a way to survive the Icelandic wilderness – rather than any level of comfort.

'Could you fetch us some water?' He handed her the empty bottle.

'Water?'

'Yes. Go down to the river.'

Although daunted at the thought of having to go back outside into the night, alone this time, she obeyed, armed only with the head torch. The hut stood on a slope and the descent to the little river was steep. She edged her way down, taking tiny steps, as it was treacherously slippery and she was no longer wearing crampons: they had taken them off once the most difficult section of the route was behind them. The last thing she wanted was to take a tumble and slide down the slope, landing in the cold, wet snow at the bottom.

Having arrived safely on the river bank, she dipped the bottle into the icy water and waited for it to fill, then lingered a moment, sneaking the first drink. The water was pure, clear and bitterly cold, straight from the glacier, wonderfully refreshing after the long hike.

Back inside the hut again, she took off her jacket, still sweating from the climb up the slope from the river. Her companion was busy lighting candles: he had explained that there was no electricity or hot water in the hut. She joined in and soon there were ten small, flickering flames helping to dispel the gloom, though they didn't give off much warmth.

'You should put your coat back on,' he said, 'or you'll soon start feeling chilled. It's the same temperature in here as it is outside.'

She nodded but didn't immediately obey. She couldn't face pulling on the bulky jacket again, not quite yet.

He took out a stove that he called a sprittprímus in Icelandic, saying he didn't know how to translate the name, lit it and heated up some baked beans. She wolfed hers down. They were delicious accompanied by cold water from the river, and brought a warm glow to her insides, but the effects didn't last long. Little by little, the cold began creeping into her bones with the inactivity. They might as well have been sitting outside in the snow as in this unheated hut.

By the time she put on her coat again it was too late, the cold had well and truly got its claws into her. Teeth chattering, she paced to and fro in the small space, doing her best to get the circulation back in her fingers and toes.

'I'll boil some water for you,' he said. 'Would you like some tea?'

She nodded.

Each mouthful of tea sent a tiny current of warmth through her frozen body, but then the shivering would reassert itself.

Suddenly, he stood up and reached for his backpack.

'I've got . . .' he started, hesitantly, almost as if he were embarrassed. 'I've got something for you.'

She wasn't sure how to react. His voice was friendly; there was nothing to be afraid of, she felt. Had he bought a gift for her? Why? She didn't have anything for him.

He opened the backpack and started scrabbling around in it, searching for something, almost frantically.

'Sorry . . . It's in here somewhere . . . Sorry.'

She waited, rather anxiously.

Finally, he presented her with a small box, wrapped in what looked – in the gloom – like gold wrapping paper.

'Here, it's for you.' He almost stammered. 'It's just a little something I picked up, nothing much.'

'Why?' she wanted to ask, but didn't.

'Thank you,' she whispered, and accepted the box, unwrapping *it clumsily with her cold fingers. Inside was a small black box, obviously something from a jeweller's.*

'Shall I open it?' she asked, hoping the answer would be no.

'Yes, yes, go ahead.'

Inside, she saw a pair of earrings and a small ring.

What on earth was this supposed to mean?

She didn't say anything, just stared at the gifts. She hoped it wasn't an engagement ring or anything like that. But no, of course it couldn't be . . .

She looked up. He was watching her.

'Sorry, it was just something I saw at the shopping centre, when I was buying stuff for the trip. I thought you might need something nice, you know. You can take it back to the shop if you like, get something else, a bracelet, shoes, whatever . . . you know.'

'Thanks,' she replied, and an awkward silence ensued.

'We'll crack on early tomorrow morning,' he said, hastily changing the subject. 'Better get a good night's sleep.'

VII

'I hope you learned something useful,' said Ólíver, giving Hulda a patronizing smile. 'If there's nothing else, I've got other work I need to be getting on with.'

Ignoring his hint, Hulda asked: 'Do you know anything about a Russian girl who vanished from the asylum-seekers' hostel last year?'

'Vanished? Well . . . yes, now you come to mention it, I remember we did issue an appeal for information about a missing asylum-seeker. A girl. Though I don't remember where she was from.'

'Could you look it up?'

Ólíver rolled his eyes. 'Yes, I suppose so. Give me your phone number and, when I get a minute, I'll let you know.' He bestowed on her the same infuriatingly condescending smile.

'Could you look it up now?' Hulda barked, in a tone of such sharp authority that he jumped.

'Now? Er, all right, I suppose . . .'

He sat down in front of the computer with a long-suffering air.

After a bit of tapping and clicking, he announced: 'Yes, she was Russian.'

'Katja?' Hulda asked.

He peered at the screen. 'Yes, that's right.'

'What happened?'

'Give me a chance to read it,' he said irritably.

Hulda sighed.

'Yes, seems we lost her,' he confirmed at last.

'You lost her?' Hulda echoed, scandalized by this choice of word.

'Yes, she never came back to the hostel. It happens, though not often. Sometimes it's a misunderstanding, sometimes they try and make a break for it, forgetting we live on an island. They always turn up again.' After a moment, he qualified this: 'Almost always.'

'But not her?'

'No, actually. Not yet, at any rate. But we'll find her.'

'It's been over a year. Are you still optimistic about that?'

'Well, I wasn't handling the case, so I wouldn't know.'

'Who is supposed to be handling it, then?' Hulda asked impatiently.

Óliver shook his head. 'It doesn't look like anyone's handling it, not directly. The file's still open. She's bound to turn up eventually.'

Hulda nodded. 'I see.'

'Maybe she's left the country,' he suggested, looking hopeful. 'By sea? Who knows? That would take care of the problem, so to speak.' He grinned.

'Did they search for her?'

'Not in any systematic way, as far as I can see. We did ask around, but there were no real leads.'

'Don't tell me: no one was particularly bothered about finding her because there were other, more pressing matters to be getting on with?'

'You could put it like that,' Óliver replied, not even having the grace to look ashamed. Though, to give him his due, he had at least begun to take her more seriously. Maybe she had been a bit hard on Óliver; she wasn't usually this rude, but the last couple of days had been extremely trying.

'You couldn't possibly give me a lift, could you?' she asked, more politely than before. She was still tired and aware of a dull throbbing behind her eyes.

'Where to?'

'To the cove where Elena's body was found. What's it called again? Flekkuvík?'

Óliver looked as if he were about to refuse, but she backed up her request with a ferocious scowl to show that she wouldn't take no for an answer. In the end, he agreed with bad grace. 'OK, let's get a move on, then.'

VIII

He climbed into the bunk directly above hers. Though the proximity made her deeply uncomfortable, there wasn't much she could do about it.

She had placed one of the candles on the chair beside the bed to give herself a little light. Their head torches were lying on the table where he had put them after switching them off, insisting that they needed to spare the batteries. She struggled into her sleeping bag, no easy task when bundled up in a thick jumper and woollen underwear, and wriggled down as far as she could. Then she blew out the candle, and the blackness closed in, relieved only, after a moment, by the faint grey outlines of the windows.

God, she was so cold, so terribly cold. The chill seemed to spread through her whole body. She tried to close the neck of her sleeping bag, clutching it tightly around her so the heat wouldn't escape, and finally resorted to tucking her head inside as well, closing the gap until there was only a tiny opening for her nose and mouth. Yet even then she couldn't get warm.

Normally, she was quick to drop off, but not here, in these alien surroundings. She lay, waiting for sleep to come, trying in vain to conquer her sense of suffocation.

IX

Ten minutes after leaving Keflavík, they took the turn-off to Vatnsleysuströnd.

'Just five minutes further along the coast,' said Ólíver, heaving a sigh. 'And after that you'll have a bit of a hike down to the sea, if you're sure you can be bothered.'

'*We*'ll have a hike, you mean,' said Hulda, as if nothing could be more natural. 'You're coming with me to show me the spot.'

At this, Ólíver gave a resigned nod.

He pulled up beside a track that looked as if it led down to the shore. It had been blocked off with a pile of rocks. 'This is as far as we can go by car,' he announced. 'There's no way round the barrier.'

The cove was further away than Hulda had expected, and the weather was lousy, too. Was she really going to put herself through this ordeal?

'How long will it take us to walk there?' she asked doubtfully.

Ólíver gave her a measuring look, his expression

betraying what he was thinking: how fast could an old woman like her be expected to move?

'Quarter of an hour either way, give or take,' he guessed, then, with a glance at his watch, added: 'Look, I really haven't got time for this and, anyway, it's not like there's anything to see down there.'

It was his reaction that tipped the scales. He was annoying her so much – though, in fairness, that might be partly the fault of her hangover – that she decided she was damn well going to drag him all the way down to the sea.

'We'll just have to make the best of it,' she said briskly, getting out of the car and setting off down the track. A glance over her shoulder revealed that Ólíver was following, albeit reluctantly. It was still drizzling and the wind was gusting hard here by the coast, but she found the effect invigorating. With any luck, it would blow away the cobwebs and, with them, the remnants of her headache. Being close to the sea improved her mood, too: she could feel her tension easing with every step. They trudged along the rough stony track, heads down into the wind, surrounded on either side by the moss-carpeted lava-field, which possessed its own brand of desolate beauty. Apart from the odd bird flying overhead, she and Ólíver were the only moving figures in the landscape. You'd never guess that there were farms not far off, since this area was sufficiently out of the way that you could be quite alone here. As she walked, Hulda wondered what in the world Elena had been doing in such a lonely spot: had she come here of her own accord and died by accident? Had she taken her own life, or had she been lured here and murdered by some person unknown?

'You didn't come across a vehicle out here, did you?' Hulda asked, raising her voice to be heard over the wind.

'What? No,' grunted Óliver, his hunched shoulders and sour expression conveying the message that he had more important things to take care of than trekking down to the shore with some old bag from Reykjavík CID.

They must be more than twenty kilometres from the hostel in Njardvík, Hulda reflected: not what you would call within easy walking distance. In this, as in other respects, Alexander's report had been deficient, failing to pinpoint exactly where the body had been found. Someone must have given Elena a lift – it stood to reason. And surely it was significant that the final stretch down to the sea was impassable to vehicles, though Alexander had omitted that detail, too.

'Was this track closed to traffic recently?' Hulda asked.

'Oh, no, that happened ages ago. No one lives here now. There's nothing out this way but a couple of derelict buildings.'

'So it's unlikely that someone would have lugged a dead body down to the beach?'

'Are you crazy? She must have died in the cove. If you ask me, it was an accident or suicide. You're wasting your time trying to solve a crime that was never committed,' he added bluntly. 'There are more than enough urgent cases to be getting on with.'

The scenery was bleak and inhospitable; only the odd hardy plant clinging on here and there, and a lone, skeletal tree.

It didn't take them long to reach the buildings, which were unmistakeably derelict. One, a two-storey house, was nothing more than a hollow shell: its twin-gabled roof still intact but the grey concrete blocks of its walls stripped bare by the elements, its windows and doors gaping holes so you could see right through it. The other house was a smaller, single-storey affair, with a red roof and peeling white paint on its walls. Once they were beside them, Hulda paused to take stock of their surroundings, noticing that they weren't overlooked by any human habitation. Even the police car parked up by the road was out of sight. More than ever, she felt convinced that Elena had been murdered in this godforsaken spot, with no witnesses. *What on earth were you doing out here, Elena?* she asked herself again. *And who were you with?*

If it was lonely and inhospitable now in May, what would it have been like when Elena came here in the dead of winter? What had been going through her mind? Did she have any inkling of what was going to happen? It was important to remember that she had just learned that she would be allowed to stay in Iceland. She must have been over the moon and perhaps this had made her more careless than usual, so she didn't perceive the risk from her companion until . . .

'It was sheer chance that the body was found so soon,' Ólíver said, interrupting her train of thought. 'Not many people come down here, especially not in winter, but a group of walkers stumbled on her. They rang the police, and me and my partner attended the scene.'

No sooner had he spoken than the cove came into view.

Although not large, it was beautiful in an austere sort of way and the sea had an air of tranquillity, in spite of the buffeting gale. Hulda experienced a momentary sense of well-being, the sight and smell of the sea transporting her for an instant back to their old home on Álftanes, to the bosom of her family, in the days before disaster fell. Then the feeling passed and her thoughts returned to Elena, who must have stood in this same spot more than a year ago, seen the same view, perhaps experienced the same sense of peace.

'They found her lying face down on the beach. She had head injuries, though there's no way of knowing exactly how she got them. Probably fell, banged her head and knocked herself out. The cause of death was drowning.'

Hulda started to pick her way gingerly over the slippery rocks towards the water's edge, feeling a need to get as close to Elena as possible, though her body was long gone.

'For Christ's sake, be careful!' Óliver shouted. 'I'm not carrying you back to the car if you break a leg.'

Hulda stopped. This was probably far enough. She could picture Elena lying there in the shallow water. The sea was so ruthless: giving life to the Icelanders, but exacting a terrible price. She gazed out over Faxaflói bay towards the great, snow-capped bulk of Mount Esja, her heart bleeding not just for Elena but for herself. She missed her old life, the good old days, and although she had gained a new friend in Pétur, she felt so utterly alone in the world. The feeling had never been stronger than in that moment.

X

'Well, that was a waste of time,' Ólíver grumbled as they got back into the squad car.

'I wouldn't be so sure about that,' Hulda said.

'Where did you leave your car? At the police station?'

'I . . . didn't come by car,' she admitted, a little sheepishly, trying to pretend this was a perfectly normal way of working.

She thought she detected a sly grin on Ólíver's face.

'Should I drive you back to Reykjavík?' he offered, with no great enthusiasm. 'It's not that far now that we've already come all this way.'

'Thanks, but I need to drop by the hostel in Njardvík. It would be great if you could give me a lift there instead.'

'Right you are,' he said.

Although the rain had temporarily let up, the clouds were still hanging low over Keflavík, threatening another downpour any minute.

'Thanks very much for your help,' said Hulda once they had reached their destination, and hurriedly exited the car. She watched as Ólíver drove off.

Elena's last dwelling place.

In the short time that had passed since Hulda had decided to delve into Elena's death, she had developed a strong feeling of connection to the young woman. And now, as she stood outside the hostel in the sudden spring cloudburst, the feeling was stronger than ever. She couldn't give up now, not when all her instincts told her she was closing in on the truth. But she was afraid that this one day, her last day, wouldn't be enough.

As it turned out, she was in luck. Dóra was sitting at the reception desk, absorbed in a newspaper.

'Hello again,' Hulda said.

Dóra looked up. 'Oh, hi there. Back again?'

'Yes. I just need a quick word with you. Any news?'

'News? No, there's never any news here.' Dóra smiled and closed the paper. 'New people, yes, but always the same old routine. Or were you talking about, you know, something to do with Elena?'

'I was, actually.'

'No, no news there. How are you getting on with your investigation thingy?'

'Getting there, slowly,' Hulda said. 'Look, could we sit down for a minute and have a chat?'

'Sure, pull up a seat, there's a stool by the phone.' Dóra gestured to a table near the reception desk on which there was an old-fashioned desk phone and next to it a bound copy of the telephone directory, a rare sight in this day and age.

'Actually, I was thinking of somewhere, well, a little more private,' said Hulda.

'Oh, none of the residents understand Icelandic. And I'd rather not leave reception unmanned, if I can help it. We've already been over this so thoroughly I'm assuming it won't take long?'

'No, it shouldn't,' said Hulda, giving in. Bringing over the telephone stool, she sat down, facing Dóra across the reception desk.

'Tell me about Katja.'

'Katja? The one who did a runner?'

'Exactly.'

'Yes, I remember her. Russian, like Elena. They were good friends, I think. Then one day she simply vanished.'

'Was her disappearance investigated?'

'I expect so. A policeman came round asking questions, but I couldn't tell him anything. I thought maybe she'd been delayed somewhere, but she never turned up again. I don't know if they ever found her, but she certainly never came back here.'

'She's still missing.'

'Oh, right. I always got on well with her. Hope she's OK, wherever she is.'

'Did anyone ever link her disappearance to Elena's death?'

'Well, that was some time later.' Dóra looked thoughtful. 'But, no, I don't think so. And I didn't mention it when your friend came round to interview me about Elena.'

'Alexander?'

'Yeah. He wasn't exactly what you'd call keen. Didn't

seem that interested in the case. You strike me as much more energetic.' Dóra smiled. 'If someone killed me, I'd definitely rather you were on the case.'

Hulda didn't smile at the black humour. 'Yesterday,' she said, 'you told me Elena had got into a four-by-four with a stranger.'

'Uhuh,' Dóra confirmed.

'Short, fat and ugly,' you said.

'That's right.'

'Well, yesterday evening, I met a man who's indirectly linked to the case, so it's possible he met Elena at some point. He has access to a four-by-four, too.' Hulda was reminded of Dóra's comment about all off-roaders looking the same to her. Perhaps that was because she had seen the same vehicle more than once; perhaps Baldur had fetched Elena in his brother Albert's car. She'd soon find out. Hulda started rummaging in her bag for her phone. When she couldn't immediately find it, she was struck by the horrible thought that she might have forgotten it at home, as it now dawned on her that she hadn't checked it all morning.

'Sorry,' she mumbled. 'Just a sec.'

Ah, there it was. Hulda let out a sigh of relief. 'The thing is, I've got a photo of him here somewhere. Let me see . . .'

Nothing happened. Was the battery out of juice? Damn.

'You don't happen to have a charger for one of these, do you?' she asked Dóra. 'That fits this . . .' She indicated the power jack.

'Can I have a look?' Dóra took the phone, pressed a

button and it made a sudden noise. 'You had it switched off. Here you go.'

At that moment, Hulda had a vague recollection of turning off her phone the night before. 'Sorry,' she said, her face reddening. Everything was going wrong today.

As she was searching for the picture the phone started making a shrill bleeping to indicate an incoming text message. Then it did it again and again and again.

'What on earth's going on?' Hulda said aloud, speaking to herself rather than to Dóra. The messages opened one after another on her screen.

CALL ME NOW

CALL ME IMMEDIATELY!

GET DOWN TO THE STATION NOW!

HULDA, CALL ME RIGHT NOW!

The texts were all from her boss, Magnús. And there was one from Alexander, too: 'Hulda, can you call me? I want to talk to you about the investigation. There's really no need to reopen it.' She decided not to reply to Alexander, or to call him.

But she couldn't ignore Magnús's texts. *What the hell was going on?*

Not that she gave a damn.

'One minute, Dóra. I need to make a quick call.' Her heart pounding, Hulda selected Magnús's number but then dithered a moment. Did she really want to talk to him? Was there any way he could have good news for her? And if not, what on earth could he want? For months, he had barely spoken to her, just left her to get on with her cases without showing the slightest interest in them. But now that he had fired her – or as good as – he was suddenly desperate to get in touch with her. Could she have stepped on someone else's toes?

She braced herself and pressed the call button.

Magnús picked up at the second ring. That in itself was unusual.

'Hulda, where the hell have you been? For fuck's sake!' She had often seen him lose his temper but, hearing his voice now, she realized she had never known him seriously enraged before.

She drew a deep breath. 'I drove out to Reykjanes to see where Elena's body was found and follow up a couple of leads. You asked me to carry on with the case today.'

'*Asked* you? I *let* you: there's a difference. And *leads*, you say? You're on some wild-bloody-goose chase, Hulda! Nobody murdered that Russian woman.'

'Actually, there were two women,' Hulda chipped in.

'Two? What do you mean? Anyway, that's irrelevant. You're to get yourself over here right now. Do you hear!'

'Is something wrong?'

'You bet your life something's wrong. Get your arse over here right now. We need to talk.'

He hung up. He had often treated her unfairly, she felt, but never had he been so downright rude. Something was seriously wrong.

Hulda sat at the reception desk, feeling shell-shocked. Not knowing what had happened was killing her. All she could think of was that it must have something to do with Áki. Had she unwittingly wrecked her colleagues' investigation? If so, why couldn't he have told her over the phone?

Finding her voice at last, her face burning, Hulda said: 'Afraid I've got to dash.'

Dóra nodded. 'Yes, I got the feeling you might. He didn't sound too happy, whoever he was!'

Hulda forced out a smile. 'No.'

'But what was it you wanted to ask me?'

'What? Oh, of course.' Hulda lowered her gaze to her phone and eventually located the photograph of Baldur Albertsson. 'It's a bit out of focus, but could this have been the man in the four-by-four?'

Dóra peered briefly at the phone then gave an emphatic nod.

Hulda stared at her, completely thrown.

'That's him,' said Dóra. 'Without a shadow of a doubt.'

XI

She awoke with a gasp.

It was impossible to breathe, she was suffocating. It took her several moments to work out where she was: cocooned in a sleeping bag in a freezing hut in the middle of the night.

The cold was so intense that it had blocked her nose, which is why she was having difficulty breathing. For a moment, she felt trapped in the sleeping bag and scrabbled frantically to widen the opening, feeling close to hysteria. She had to get her head free so she could snatch some air.

Finally, she succeeded.

Sitting up a little, she tried to calm down, to slow the frantic beating of her heart.

Her coat, which she was using as a pillow, had become uncomfortably creased. She refolded it to make it as soft as possible then lay down again, pulling her sleeping bag up to her chin, leaving her head uncovered this time, and concentrated on trying to get back to sleep.

XII

Hulda shelled out for a taxi back to Reykjavík: CID could pay. She supposed she could have rung Óliver and accepted his offer but that would have taken more time and she was in a hurry.

To her intense relief, the driver who picked her up showed no propensity to chat, leaving her free to think. Halfway back to Reykjavík, she realized she had failed to keep her word to Amena: she had promised to tell Óliver that she had helped the police, but then forgotten to do so, too preoccupied with her own problems. She had felt so sorry for herself all day, but now she felt a sense of guilt. Poor Amena didn't have many allies in this country, and Hulda could have done something to help her, a small favour. She had been entirely focused on saving Elena, though it was too late for her. But Amena was still alive and Hulda had a chance to right this wrong; she resolved to call Óliver later, just not right now.

The sky was brightening: with any luck, they'd leave the drizzle behind on Reykjanes.

With her nerves still jangling from her phone conversation with Magnús, there was no chance of grabbing a nap during the drive. The adrenaline was pumping through her veins and her mind was racing. She had no idea what was coming but, prepared for the worst, decided she'd better ring Pétur.

'Hulda, what an unexpected pleasure,' he said, sounding as upbeat as ever. 'How are things?'

'Busy, actually,' she said. It was a relief to hear a friendly voice and know that, in him, she had found someone she could trust, someone she could really talk to. It was a heart-warming feeling.

'I'm looking forward to this evening. I've booked a table.'

'Yes, about that . . . is there any way we could postpone it till tomorrow? I'm not quite sure how my day's going to pan out.'

'Oh, I see.' The disappointment was clear in his voice. 'No problem.'

'Could I maybe ring you once I'm free? We could grab a bite to eat then.'

'Yes, that sounds good. But we can't postpone till tomorrow: it'll have to be the day after.'

'What?'

'Dinner at Hótel Holt. We can't postpone it till tomorrow because we're climbing Esja tomorrow evening. Had you forgotten?'

'Oh, yes, of course, so we are.' At the thought, she was filled with a surge of happy anticipation, looking forward both to the hike and to spending time with Pétur.

'I'll hear from you later, then,' Pétur said.

'Yes, I'm hoping I won't be too late,' Hulda replied, grateful that he had reacted so well to the last-minute change of plans.

They rang off and Hulda was left alone with her thoughts again. Part of her wanted to give the taxi driver a different destination, chicken out of the coming meeting with Magnús. Her complete ignorance of what he wanted to see her about only made matters worse. If only she could go home, relax, recover her composure and never darken the doors of CID again. Never be forced to deal with her useless boss, never have to listen to his reprimands. But that would mean abandoning Elena to her fate and perhaps allowing her killer to walk free.

She knew only too well that this wasn't an option: she was someone who stuck to her guns, always had done. So she sat there in silence as the taxi ate up the kilometres, the lava-fields of Reykjanes giving way to the suburbs of Reykjavík, a mixture of apartment blocks and large detached houses with back gardens where families might be enjoying a barbecue, now that the weather was cheering up; the kind of life that Hulda had lost.

As soon as she walked into the station, preparing herself mentally for the coming storm, it struck her: something had changed. You could have cut the atmosphere with a knife. She made a beeline for Magnús's office, looking neither left nor right, avoiding her colleagues' eyes. For once, though, he wasn't there. At a loss, Hulda looked around awkwardly, before deciding to try his second-in-command, who occupied the smaller office next door. Yet another young man whose rise through the ranks had been more meteoric than Hulda would have ever dreamed possible.

She was spared the effort of explaining her business. He started talking the moment he saw her, and it was plain from his expression that he didn't envy her the impending encounter. 'Maggi's waiting for you in the meeting room.' He told her which one, shaking his head as if to imply that the battle Hulda was about to engage in was already lost.

She made her way to meet her doom with dreamlike slowness, like a condemned prisoner on her way to the gallows, still completely in the dark about what was going on.

Magnús was alone in the room. From the look on his face it was painfully obvious that he was in a foul mood. Before she could even greet him, he asked curtly: 'Have you spoken to anyone?'

'Spoken to anyone?' she echoed, confused.

'About what happened last night.'

'I haven't a clue what happened, I'm afraid,' she said.

'Good. Sit down.'

She took a seat across the table from Magnús. There were some papers in front of him, but Hulda's eyesight wasn't what it used to be and she couldn't make them out.

'Emma Margeirsdóttir,' he said slowly, after a long pause, his eyes resting on the papers.

Hulda's blood ran cold when she heard the name.

'You know who she is, don't you?'

'Oh my God, has something happened to her?' Hulda asked, in a voice close to breaking.

'You've met her, haven't you?'

'Yes, of course. But you knew that. I'd already told you.'

'Quite.' He nodded and allowed a silence to develop. And drag on. He was clearly hoping to entrap Hulda with her own tactics, but she wasn't going to fall for that; she was determined to force him to make the next move.

In the end, he caved in first. 'You questioned her, didn't you?'

'Yes, that's right.'

'And you told me, if memory serves, that nothing of interest had emerged from the interview.'

Hulda nodded, feeling herself break out in a sweat. She wasn't used to being on the receiving end of an interrogation, and you could hardly call this anything else.

'"Nowhere near solving it" – those were your exact words, weren't they?'

Again, she nodded. Magnús waited for her to answer and, this time, she couldn't stand the pressure: 'That's right.'

After a further pause, Magnús said, on a slightly gentler note than before: 'You know, I'm a little surprised at you, Hulda.'

'Why?'

'I thought you were one of the best in the business. In fact, I know you are. You've proved that repeatedly over the years.'

Hulda waited, unsure how to react to this, one of the first and only compliments he'd ever given her.

'The thing is, she's confessed.'

'Confessed?' Hulda couldn't believe her ears. *Was it possible?* After all that had happened; after Hulda had risked her neck to spare the woman.

'Yes. We arrested her last night and she admitted to having knocked down that man, that bastard paedophile. Naturally, she has my sympathy, but the inescapable fact is that she ran the man down – deliberately. What do you say to that?'

'It's unbelievable,' said Hulda, striving, but no doubt failing, to strike a convincing note.

'Yes, unbelievable. But she had a powerful motive, as we both know.'

'Yes, she did.' Hulda made an effort to breathe calmly.

'She can expect to do time. And her son, well, who knows what'll happen to him? It's tough, Hulda; don't you agree?'

'Yes, of course. I really don't know what to say . . .'

'One can't help but sympathize with her.'

'Well, I suppose . . .'

'You've got a reputation for that, Hulda: for giving people the benefit of the doubt. Avoiding passing judgement. I'm aware of that much, though, sadly, we've never got to know each other as well as we might have done.'

Sadly. The hypocrisy of it.

'Did you give her an easy ride?'

'What do you mean?'

'During the interview.'

'No, far from it. I came down pretty hard on her, considering the circumstances.'

'With no result?'

'No.'

'The thing is, Hulda, there's one part I don't quite understand,' he said, drawing his brows together and employing that familiar patronizing tone he'd used so often before. 'You see, Emma claims that she confessed to you during your conversation . . .'

It was as if Magnús had lobbed a hand grenade into the room. Hulda felt herself go weak at the knees. Was there any way she could dig herself out of this? How much had Emma said? Why had she betrayed Hulda like that? It was incomprehensible.

Or was Magnús bluffing?

Fishing for the truth?

Trying to trick Hulda into admitting misconduct?

The problem was, she couldn't read him, didn't know how to play the next move. Should she make a clean breast of things or carry on lying to him and deny it?

Hulda took her time before answering. 'Well,' she said eventually, 'to tell the truth, she was very unclear. Of course, she was still in a distressed state about those pictures we found of her son. It's possible she may have thought she'd confessed to something, but that wasn't how I experienced our conversation.' She dabbed at the perspiration on her brow.

'I see.' Magnús's face remained impassive.

He was quite good at this, Hulda realized: she'd underestimated him.

'So it was all a misunderstanding between the two of you. Could that explain it?'

Hulda had the feeling that she was digging herself deeper and deeper into a hole with every question she answered. She felt uncomfortable in Magnús's office, as if she were trapped there.

'Must have been. Are you absolutely sure she did it – knocked him down, I mean? Regardless of her confession?'

'What are you implying?' he asked slowly, sounding more curious than surprised.

'Perhaps it was just a cry for attention, especially if she told you she'd already confessed before.' Hulda went on trying to brazen it out, though all she really wanted at this stage was to give in and admit everything.

'She was definitely responsible for the hit-and-run, I don't think there's any real doubt about that. But that's not the main issue here.'

'Oh?'

'She had more to tell me . . .'

At this, Hulda's heart began racing so fast she thought she might faint, and Magnús spun out the moment, as if he were enjoying watching her squirm.

'Emma told me you'd got in touch with her later that same evening, after the interview. Is that correct?'

'I don't remember. Yes, maybe, to check some details for my report.'

'Hulda, she claims you rang to tell her not to worry about her confession. That you weren't going to take it any further.' And now he raised his voice, his face like thunder. 'Is that possible, Hulda? Is there the slightest *possibility* that she's telling the truth?'

How was she supposed to respond to this? Ruin her record on the eve of her retirement, all for an act of kindness that had rebounded on her? Or continue to deny it? After all, it was Emma's word against hers.

To win time, she opted not to say anything.

'Do you know what I think, Hulda? I think you felt sorry for her. No one wastes any pity on a paedophile – not me, not you – but that doesn't mean we can take the law into our own hands. If you ask me, I think that sympathy for this woman led you to cross a line. Which I can understand, in a way.' He paused briefly, but Hulda remained obstinately mute. 'She would be facing prison, mother and son would be separated . . . I do understand. You lost your daughter, after all.'

'Keep my daughter out of this!' Hulda shouted. 'What the hell do you know about her? You don't know a thing about me and my family and you never have!' This explosion took even Hulda by surprise, but at least it succeeded in momentarily wrong-footing Magnús. He'd better not dare to drag Dimma into this again. If he did, Hulda couldn't be held responsible for her actions.

'I'm sorry, Hulda. I was just trying to put myself in your shoes.'

It was becoming all too clear that Emma had shopped her, in spite of Hulda's good intentions. The woman's betrayal was so incomprehensible that Hulda felt wounded even thinking about it. Yes, Emma had been in a highly agitated state, but that wasn't enough to excuse her behaviour. She must have had a complete meltdown when questioned by Magnús.

Only then did Hulda remember why she had switched off her phone yesterday evening. Why the hell had she drunk all that wine? Her hangover wasn't helping her cope with the pressure now. She was on the back foot in everything she did today, just when she needed to be at the peak of her powers. Perhaps age was catching up with her, she thought, before angrily rejecting the idea. She knew she was as good an officer now as she had ever been.

Emma had rung her, late at night. That should have set off alarm bells, suggesting, as it did, that she had some urgent reason for trying to get in touch. But Hulda hadn't been in the mood to talk to her. God, how she regretted that now. Perhaps Emma had wanted to consult her about turning herself in. Oh, Christ.

'This is an extremely serious matter, Hulda,' said Magnús after a weighty pause.

She still couldn't work out how she ought to react and what the repercussions of her actions might be. Surely he wasn't planning to sack her in disgrace on her last day at work?

'Are you saying that she's confessed now?' Hulda asked, aware that her question contained an acknowledgement of her mistake, without being a direct admission of guilt. 'Does it really matter what we talked about or how she interpreted the outcome?' She bit back the shameful desire to whine: *Please, be lenient. After all these years, after my long, successful career, couldn't we overlook this one little mistake?*

'You've hit the nail on the head there, Hulda. In normal circumstances, I don't suppose I'd have made a big deal out of this, seeing as you're leaving anyway and it's a difficult time for you. An error of judgement, no harm done.'

In normal circumstances? What was he trying to tell her?

'But it gets worse. Emma went down to the National Hospital last night. I gather she's worked for the health service in the past and is currently employed at a nursing home.'

'The National Hospital?'

'Yes, apparently, it wasn't too difficult: there's not much security, she knew her way around and, whenever she encountered a locked door, she managed to blag her way through by flashing her work ID.'

Suspecting now where this was leading, Hulda started to feel sick.

'It didn't take her long to track down the paedophile's ward. They were keeping him in an induced coma, but I understand that he was making satisfactory progress.' Magnús paused, no doubt catching the look of horror on Hulda's face, then resumed his account: 'She picked up a pillow and held it over the man's face.'

Hulda was too terrified to ask what had happened next. She waited, caught in an agony of hope and fear.

'He's dead.'

'She killed him?' Hulda asked incredulously, though she had already guessed as much.

'She killed him, Hulda. Then immediately turned herself in. Told us the whole sorry story. That she'd run him down in her car because of what he'd done to her son. She'd meant to kill him then, not just for revenge but to stop him doing the same thing to someone else's child. You went to interview her at work, didn't you? And immediately saw through her denials. She said you gave her the third degree and, in the end, she caved in and admitted what she'd done. It was a relief, she said. And she also said . . .' He dropped his eyes to the papers in front of him and referred to Emma's statement: 'That she was relieved to get it off her chest. There was no way she could live with what she'd done. Following your visit, she expected to be arrested any minute, but later that evening you rang her up and told her you were going to let her off. She was stunned – grateful, of course, but at the same time disappointed. Her guilt was weighing so heavily on her that she decided she had no choice but to confess. So she rang your number.'

Hulda flinched. The late-night phone call.

'But you didn't answer.'

Hulda shook her head, shattered. 'No, I was busy,' she whispered. *Why the hell hadn't she picked up?*

Magnús went on turning the knife. 'She was in a bad state last night and couldn't think straight. Felt she had no future, nothing but darkness ahead, so she might as well finish what she'd started. Achieve something worth-while. You know, you could have stopped her last night, Hulda.'

She nodded, her throat too constricted to make a sound.

'To say nothing of the gross misconduct you showed

by covering up for her. More than misconduct – as you're perfectly aware, Hulda, you broke the law, obstructed the course of justice.'

But my intentions were good, she thought to herself. The law wasn't the sole arbiter of right and wrong. Sometimes you had to look at the bigger picture. She had no illusions; she was well aware of how dangerous it was for someone in her position to think like that. After all, she had sworn an oath to uphold the law. But this wasn't the first time she had broken it on the pretext that, in certain circumstances, such behaviour was justified. The only difference was that, this time, she had been found out. A man was dead, and it was partly her fault. She suddenly felt violently sick, yet she couldn't summon up any grief for the paedophile's death. Perhaps saying he had deserved to die would be going too far, but she was certain that the world was a better, safer place without him.

'Can't we . . . ?' She broke off, unable to finish the sentence. For the second time in her life, her world was collapsing around her. First when Dimma had died, now this. Her reputation, her exemplary record at work, all of it about to go up in smoke. And what was worse: she could be facing charges. Could she bear to end up in the dock after her long career in the police? Go to prison . . . ? And what about Pétur, what would he say? She had a horrible fear that the future, which she had belatedly begun to look forward to, was about to slip out of her grasp.

Magnús sat without moving or speaking, his eyes fixed on Hulda. The silence grew so oppressive that she wanted to scream; she was feeling too drained for anything else.

'You can't imagine how difficult this is for me, Hulda,' he said at last. 'How disappointed I am. I've always respected you.'

Sceptical though she was about that, she didn't contradict him.

'You're a role model for so many of us here in CID. And you've paved the way for so many others, like Karen. You've put me in an impossible position, Hulda.'

Hulda wasn't sure how to take this. Was Magnús being sincere? She hoped so, but if he was, that would mean she had misread the situation all these years, underestimated the respect she actually commanded among her colleagues.

She bowed her head in defeat; all the fight had gone out of her.

'I'm furious, make no mistake, but I'm not going to waste time yelling at you: it's far too serious for that. More than anything, I'm devastated,' he went on, and to Hulda's amazement, it sounded as though he meant it. 'I've often stuck up for you when there was talk of replacing you or transferring you to another department. You're slow but persistent, old school, and not everyone appreciates that. But you get results.'

She wasn't sure whether to believe this; she had never felt she got any real support from Magnús, not once. But she had certainly achieved results over the years, leading investigations in some high-profile cases. She remembered two of them in particular: a death on a small island off the south coast of Iceland, where four friends had intended to spend a quiet weekend; and the horrible

events at an isolated farm in the eastern part of the country, that Christmas in 1987 – the Christmas when Dimma
had died. Both cases had been very difficult for her emo-
tionally, and the events often came back to haunt her.

'Thank you,' she muttered to Magnús, so low as to be
almost inaudible.

'We'll try to keep this quiet, Hulda, for both our sakes.
I haven't shared any of the details with your colleagues. It
would be a shame for you to end your career in disgrace,
though it'll almost certainly come out later if you face
charges. But we'll cross that bridge when we come to it.
I'll pass the matter on to the State Prosecutor on Monday
and, after that, it'll be out of my hands. I can't make it disappear, Hulda, you must understand that. But we'll try to
limit the damage.'

She nodded in humble gratitude. It didn't cross her
mind to deny it, to go on lying. The game was up.

'Of course, you'll have to quit your duties immediately –
there'll be no more latitude. Have you cleared your office?'

She shook her head dumbly.

'Then I'll get someone to do it for you and send the
stuff round to your flat, OK?'

'OK.'

'By the way, what happened about the Russian
asylum-seeker?'

Hulda was fighting to stop herself breaking down. She
couldn't end her career like this: sixty-four years old, in
floods of tears on her last day at work. Clearing her throat,
she said hoarsely: 'I'm still working on it. There were two
of them.'

'Yes, you mentioned that on the phone earlier. What did you mean?'

'There was a Russian girl called Katja who went missing over a year ago. Then Elena died. The two girls were best friends. I doubt Alexander made the connection.'

'*Are* they connected?'

'I don't know, but it needs checking out.'

'You're right.' He thought for a bit then said: 'Could you write a report and email it to me when you get a moment? I'll take a look at it myself as soon as I have time.'

His tone of voice betrayed him. She didn't believe him for a minute, but she appreciated the gesture.

'Yes, sure, I'll do that.'

He rose to his feet, holding out his hand, and she shook it without a word.

'It was a privilege working with you, Hulda. You were an outstanding cop.' He paused, then added: 'It's a pity it had to end like this.'

XIII

She woke again with a start, sensing that it was still the middle of the night.

At first, she thought it was the cold that had woken her, and it was true that she was freezing, not just her head but her whole body. Only then did it dawn on her that her sleeping bag was unzipped.

Her companion had moved down from the top bunk and climbed into hers, and was now lying beside her, one hand burrowing inside her underwear.

Frantic with terror, she tried to shove him off, but she was so cold that her limbs wouldn't obey. He pulled her against him, kissing her, while she struggled with all the strength she could muster to push him away.

'Cut it out,' he snarled. 'We both knew what would happen — what I meant by inviting you away for the weekend. I've seen how you look at me. Don't start acting all coy, for fuck's sake.'

She heard him in stunned disbelief.

Next moment, she was screaming at the top of her lungs, louder than she had ever screamed in her life.

He didn't even bother to clamp a hand over her mouth.

XIV

Hulda stood outside the police station on Hverfisgata, frozen into immobility. A few colleagues said hello as they walked past, but she was incapable of returning their greetings. She just stood there, staring unseeingly into space.

It was as if her life had been brought to a full stop: she couldn't look forward, couldn't picture what tomorrow might bring. Her greatest need now was to talk to Pétur, but she couldn't bring herself to call him. Not yet.

Eventually finding the will to move, she set off slowly round the corner of the building and kept walking in the direction of the sea. Although the sun had broken free of the clouds, she was met by a stiff breeze when she reached the coast road. She crossed it, heedless of the traffic, and took a seat on a bench, gazing out across the bay towards the panorama of mountains. She never tired of this view. All those summits she had conquered in her time: Esja, Skardsheidi, Akrafjall. The breathtaking beauty had a calming effect, soothing her, taking her back to some of her happiest moments. But it also brought back images of Elena washed up in the cove. The sea giveth and the sea taketh away.

Once again, Hulda felt the crushing weight of her loneliness.

She had so much on her conscience.

Her thoughts returned to Elena. Could she be the key? The way by which she could earn a kind of absolution? Restore her honour, to some degree? Could she salvage something from the wreckage of her life by solving this case? If nothing else, to feel more reconciled to herself?

The restless waters of Faxaflói bay supplied no answers, but perhaps they brought a tiny glint of hope. She had assured Magnús she was abandoning her inquiry, but what were the chances of his finding out if she continued working on it for the rest of the day? Made full use of her last few hours on the job? There were two leads she still had to follow up. Who would it hurt if she went ahead? It would mean having to lie, pretend she was still in the police, but it was unlikely anyone would question the fact.

Yes, she had to do it. Just for today. It was her last chance. It would provide the necessary distraction until she could summon up the courage to face Pétur this evening.

XV

'No one can hear you,' he said, laughing as he wrestled with her long johns, trying to pull them down.

It was then that she acquired an extra burst of strength from somewhere, in spite of the numbing cold, and managed to shove him away so hard that he fell off the bed on to the floor.

She leapt out of the bunk, blind in the gloom, aware that her only chance was to get out of the hut and run away into the snow, find somewhere to hide in the vast, empty landscape. As unrealistic as the idea was, she had to try. In that instant, she spotted the faint gleam of the ice axe that he had untied from her rucksack and placed by the door.

By some miracle, she managed to reach it first.

XVI

Hulda knocked on Albert's door. She was hoping to speak to his brother and find out whether he had taken Elena for a drive somewhere in a four-by-four. To her surprise, the lawyer answered the door himself, though it was not yet four in the afternoon.

'Hulda?' he said, a little taken aback.

'Albert, I just knocked on the off-chance . . .'

'Right, right, I came home early for once, as there wasn't much on.' He seemed embarrassed and a little shifty, as if business might not be going that well. 'Didn't you get the papers? Baldur told me you dropped by yesterday evening to pick them up.'

'Oh, yes, I've got them. But they're all in Russian, so I haven't been able to glean anything from them yet.'

'Yes, I thought they were, but, you never know, there might be something useful in there. Let's hope you can get justice for the poor woman. She was my client, after all.'

'Actually, I was hoping to have another quick word with your brother.'

'With my brother?' Evidently, this was the last thing Albert was expecting to hear.

'Yes . . . He, um, there was something he happened to mention yesterday,' she lied clumsily, cursing herself for not having come up with a better excuse, but then she hadn't been expecting to run into Albert, 'that I just wanted him to clarify.'

'What on earth has he been telling you? Something to do with Elena?'

'No, well, yes, not directly. It's a bit hard to explain.'

'To do with me, then?' Albert's voice sharpened.

'What? Of course not, nothing like that. Is he in?'

'No, he isn't. He managed to pick up a house-painting job today, so he won't be home for a while yet.'

'Could you ask him to give me a ring when he does get in?'

Albert appeared unsure how to react to this request, but eventually said: 'Yes, yes, of course. I'll do that. I'll call you at the station.'

'No, call the mobile, you've got my number,' Hulda said hurriedly, and smiled.

Albert briefly returned her smile then quickly closed the door.

XVII

Since access to the services of an official police translator was now denied to her, the obvious answer was to see if Bjartur could help. Hulda got back in her car and headed out to the interpreter's place in the west of town. It would be her final port of call, unless something significant turned up in the papers. While part of her clung to this hope, the realization was growing that she would be grateful to let it go and have a rest at last.

Her phone rang and she pulled over to answer. It was Magnús again.

'Hulda,' he said, sounding grave.

'Yes.' She braced herself.

'I didn't want to burden you with anything else today but there's something I forgot to mention: they arrested Áki this morning.'

'Really?' Her spirits rose a little. 'For running a prostitution ring?'

'Among other things, but the downside is that they were forced to bring the whole operation forward and it's ended up being a bit of a rush job – all because you went and interviewed him without permission.'

Hulda swore under her breath.

'And there's a risk he'll have been busy destroying records in the interim, which is a bugger. You'd better be prepared for them to call you about your conversation with him. They'll want to know if he gave anything away, what information you were acting on . . .'

Hulda sighed. 'Yes, OK . . . Though I've nothing new to give them.'

'Then I'm afraid you'll just have to put up with the hassle. This whole thing's a total fiasco, but don't let it get to you.'

Any more than it already has, she thought as she rang off. Hulda felt truly guilty over having potentially ruined her colleagues' investigation, knowing how much effort they must have put into it.

She hated making mistakes.

She *really* hated making mistakes.

When she was young, doing her school homework, her grandmother used to be constantly looking over her shoulder, checking every answer, every composition, whether it was grammar, maths, geography, history . . . And her criticisms had often been both harsh and unfair, Hulda felt. Time and time again, her grandmother had told her that she had to do better, that she was too slow, that she had to outperform the boys to have any chance of succeeding in life. She had often been brought to tears by these exchanges.

Only as an adult had she learned the concept of

constructive criticism, something completely alien to her grandmother.

And now, yet again, she felt the shame of having made a mistake.

She could do better than this.

XVIII

This time, Hulda didn't waste time going to the house but marched straight round to Bjartur's garage and knocked on the door. As she did so, she noticed a neat sign in the window: 'Bjartur Hartmannsson, interpreter and translator.'

He answered the door quickly and looked surprised to see Hulda.

'Hello.'

'Hello, Bjartur, me again,' she said apologetically, aware that she was forever tilting at windmills, on a mission to solve a case that was almost certainly a lost cause.

'Well, well,' he said with a smile, scratching his blond thatch. 'Looks like I'm becoming an old friend of the police.'

Hulda wondered idly how old he was; she hadn't bothered to look him up but guessed that, despite his boyish appearance, he must be pushing forty. The woman – presumably his mother – who had answered the door on Hulda's first visit had looked to be around seventy.

'Plenty to do?' she asked in a friendly voice.

'Yeah, sure, well . . . not so much in the translation line, but plenty of Russian tour groups. I swear the tourist dollar's the only thing keeping Iceland afloat these days. But things are quiet today. I'm just . . . writing, you know, working on my book.'

The surge in tourism since the collapse of the Icelandic banking system – and the subsequent collapse of the Icelandic króna – was certainly helping to get the country back on track, since the tourists brought in valuable foreign currency. The outlook was a bit brighter than before, but the financial crisis had cast a long shadow, and Hulda, momentarily distracted, reflected that tourism would do little to boost her personal finances. Her job didn't pay that well, and now all she had to look forward to was a fixed income from her government pension.

'Come in,' Bjartur said, breaking into her thoughts. 'It's still a bit of a mess, I'm afraid. I haven't got round to buying a chair for visitors so you'll have to make do with the bed.' He turned red. 'I mean, you know, you'll have to sit on the bed.'

Hulda found a space free of clutter where she could park herself while Bjartur sat down in his superannuated office chair. The air in the room was unpleasantly stuffy: Hulda's unexpected arrival had given him no chance to open a window.

'Do you live out here in the garage?' she asked curiously.

'Yes, I do, actually. I sleep and work in here. It's more private, you see. Mum and Dad have the house, but I couldn't live with them any longer. It all got too much, living on top of each other like that. Unfortunately, there's no basement or I'd have moved down there, but they let me do up the garage.'

Hulda wanted to ask why he hadn't simply moved into a flat of his own but didn't like to, in case it sounded rude.

Bjartur seemed to guess the unspoken question: 'There's no point getting a flat of my own, not yet; it's way too expensive, whether you rent or buy. House prices are going through the roof and I don't have a regular income. It's all pretty hand to mouth – translation work, tour-guide gigs. Sometimes I'm rushed off my feet, especially in the summers, but often there's not enough work to go round. I'm managing to save up a bit, though. It'll all work out in the end. And Mum and Dad are getting on, so they're bound to want to downsize at some point.'

Or die, Hulda read from his expression.

'I wanted to ask you a small favour,' she said.

'Oh, yes? What's that?'

She handed him the envelope of papers Albert had passed on to her.

'It contains some documents that Elena's lawyer dug out. I don't know if there's anything of interest, but "no stone unturned", and all that.' She smiled, making light of it.

'I get you. How's the investigation going, by the way? I see you're still on the case.'

'Yes . . . sure, I'm not planning to give up,' she lied. The truth was that she would happily have abandoned it right now. Today of all days, when she was still reeling from the news Magnús had broken to her, pursuing this case was the last thing she felt like doing, though it was the only thing she had left.

There was no getting away from the fact that a man had died because of her. But he had been a child abuser, and that made it easier to square with her conscience: some crimes were quite simply unforgiveable.

And there was a good chance that she had sabotaged her colleagues' investigation into Áki's activities. Her career as a detective inspector lay in smoking ruins. No wonder she wasn't in any fit state to be working. Yet, in spite of everything, she persisted, too pig-headed to quit, caught up in a last race against time.

'Of course I'll take a look at them for you,' Bjartur said, swivelling his chair round to face the desk, where he drew the papers from the envelope and spread them out in front of him. 'Just give me a few minutes to run through them.'

'Of course.' On a sudden hunch, she added: 'Could you pay particular attention to any mentions of somebody called Katja.'

'Katja?' he queried, still poring over the pages.

'Yes, I gather she was a friend of hers.'

'OK.'

'You didn't know her? Interpret for her?'

'Nope.'

'The thing is, she went missing.'

'Went missing?'

'Well, either that or did a disappearing act. She was a Russian asylum-seeker, too, and it occurred to me that the cases might be linked.'

'OK. Nothing yet. This first document is just some kind of residence certificate from Russia; she must have brought it with her to prove her identity.'

'Oh, I see,' said Hulda, a little disappointed. She knew she was clutching at straws, but these papers were her last chance. 'Please read them carefully,' she added, as politely as she could.

'Sure.'

Bjartur read on without speaking, his back to Hulda, while she perched uncomfortably on the edge of his bed, waiting in an agony of suspense. The silence dragged out interminably until finally Bjartur showed some kind of reaction.

'Whoa,' he said, and it was evident from his tone that he'd found something unexpected. 'Whoa,' he repeated.

'What?' Hulda got up and peered over his shoulder. He was reading the last sheet of paper, which was handwritten.

'Have you found something?' she demanded impatiently.

'Well . . . I wouldn't like to . . . though . . .'

'What?' she asked, her voice sharpening. 'What does it say?'

'She's talking about a trip she made to the countryside with a friend who she refers to as K. Could it have been Katja?'

'Yes, could be, could be.' Hulda felt herself tensing with excitement. At last.

'And someone . . . I'm not sure if it's a man or a woman . . .'

'Come on, out with it . . .'

'She's used an initial again. But from the context it looks like there was a man with them.'

'What's the initial?'

'An A.'

XIX

He laughed.

'Put the axe down and we'll talk. You don't have the guts to use it, anyway.'

Beside herself with terror, she braced herself against the door, brandishing the axe in front of her with one hand while groping for the door handle with the other.

He didn't seem in the least fazed and took a step closer. Then, in one fell swoop, he was on her and had torn the axe from her hand.

For an instant, he stood quite still.

She was paralysed by fear, though all her instincts were screaming at her to get outside.

Then he lunged.

Had the axe hit her on the head? She experienced a split second of bewildered disbelief, still too numb with the cold to register what had happened.

Then, raising a hand to her scalp, she felt the hot blood seeping out.

XX

'An A?'

'Yes.'

'You don't mean . . . ?'

'That was my immediate thought, too,' said Bjartur with a nod, looking dismayed.

Hulda said it out loud: 'Albert?'

'Yes.'

'But maybe, maybe it was all perfectly harmless. Something to do with preparing their cases. Could he have been Katja's lawyer, too?'

Bjartur shrugged. 'It doesn't sound harmless, though. She's hinting at some kind of violence – this reads like an excerpt from a diary. Maybe she wanted to put it down in writing in case something happened. At least, I'm assuming Elena wrote this. She spoke very little English so, naturally, she'd have written in Russian.'

'What, and Albert came across it, ignorant of what it contained, and passed it on to me?'

'The irony,' said Bjartur. 'You know, I feel as if I'm in

267

the middle of a whodunnit. I used to read a lot of those when I was younger.' He grinned, as if relishing the role of detective's assistant.

'Christ . . .' Hulda muttered. Which way was she to turn on this one? Was it conceivable that it was Albert himself, not his brother, who had something to hide?

'Let me finish it,' said Bjartur, and bent his head over the page again, nodding as he read: 'Yes, yes.' He was really getting into the role. 'You know what?' he said, raising his eyes from the paper. 'I reckon I know where they went. It's a bit of a way, about an hour and a half's drive from Reykjavík.' He mentioned a valley that Hulda hadn't heard of, but then she was more into mountains herself: valleys didn't hold the same thrill.

Bjartur went on: 'It's odd, though, because she mentions a house, but as far as I know, the valley's un-inhabited.'

'Could you point to it on a map?' Hulda asked.

'I can do better than that: I can take you there,' he offered eagerly. 'I've got nothing else on.'

'Yes, OK. Thanks. I'll talk to Albert afterwards. Could you translate the document for me, word for word?'

'Sure, I'll tell you what it says while we're driving. Er, could we go in your car? I don't, er, I haven't got quite enough in my tank to get us there.'

Life as a translator clearly meant only just scraping by, Hulda thought, feeling a twinge of pity for the man.

She got behind the wheel of her trusty old Skoda. Bjartur climbed into the passenger seat, where he acted as navigator, in between filling her in on the contents of the handwritten account. Elena had gone on a trip to the valley in the company of two other people, a woman whose name began with a K and a man whose name began with an A. They had spent the night in a summer cabin, but the weekend had ended prematurely when the man had physically assaulted the other woman.

Although Hulda found it hard to believe that Albert could be involved, she couldn't entirely rule it out. Was it conceivable that he could have murdered both women, both Katja and Elena? And where did his brother come into it?

When her phone started ringing, she sent up a fervent prayer that it wasn't Magnús yet again. She was still in shock after their last two conversations, still hadn't managed to piece everything together. Really, she could have done with another day to wrap up this case, a day when she was feeling more herself. And perhaps, she caught herself thinking, loath though she was to admit it, perhaps she could have done with being ten years younger.

Pulling over to the side of the road, she took out her phone and answered, although the caller ID was unfamiliar.

'Hulda? Hello, this is Baldur, Baldur Albertsson. Albert's brother.'

'What? Oh, yes. Hello.' The timing seemed uncannily apt.

'Albert said you wanted a word with me ...' He sounded nervous.

'Yes, I do. It's about Elena, the Russian girl your brother was representing.'

'Yes . . .'

'Did you know her at all?'

'Me? No . . .' He hesitated, and Hulda waited. 'No . . . but I, that is, I met her once or twice. Why do you ask?'

'Would you mind telling me where you met her?'

'I collected her from Njardvík a couple of times.'

'Oh? Why was that?'

'As a favour to my brother. He needed to see her but hadn't time to go and collect her himself. He was busy with meetings or something. So I borrowed his jeep and drove over to fetch her. It's no big deal. We put it down on expenses – you know, the time it took and the cost of the petrol. That's not a problem, is it? It was all above board, even though, strictly speaking, Albert didn't do the driving himself. I help him out when I'm free – it's the least I can do in return for getting to live with him. I like to make a contribution, if I can.' Baldur's breathing sounded fast and ragged over the phone.

Was that all it amounted to? Had Baldur simply been doing his brother a favour?

'Thanks, Baldur. It's not a problem. I just wanted to check so I can eliminate you from my inquiries. Someone saw you collecting her from Njardvík and I needed to know why, that's all. Don't worry, it's absolutely fine.'

'OK, thanks,' he said. 'I . . . only, I'm not used to getting mixed up in police investigations.'

'Quite. Just as well.'

'You can say that again.'

Hulda still needed to know if Albert had also represented the other Russian girl, Katja.

'By the way,' she asked, as casually as she could, 'is your brother with you, Baldur? I have a couple of questions for him, too.'

There was a silence at the other end of the line.

'Well . . . no, he's not here.' After a hesitation, Baldur added: 'I'm not sure where he is, actually.'

'OK, Baldur, no problem. Thanks for calling.'

She tried Albert's mobile. She felt a growing sense of urgency about getting hold of him, afraid that, if he was the killer, he might be trying to leave the country or something.

There was no reply.

As she hung up, her thoughts suddenly flew to the Syrian girl, Amena. Something was niggling at the back of her mind. Some comment Amena had let slip . . . a significant detail that Hulda had overlooked the first time round. Damn it. She'd been more conscientious about taking notes in the old days, and her memory had been better then, too. It was some . . . something she'd said . . . Hulda summoned up an image of the girl in her cell. Prostitution, yes: Amena had vehemently denied that Elena had been involved in prostitution. Her denial had been convincing, too. She'd also alerted Hulda to the existence of the other Russian woman, Katja. And she'd referred to the residence permit – that Elena had been granted the right to stay . . . yes, that was it . . . it was something related to that. But what the hell was it? The memory still eluded her, remaining tantalizingly just out of reach.

'Sorry, but could I possibly borrow your phone a minute?' Bjartur asked, breaking into her thoughts before she could start the car again. 'Only, I forgot to tell my parents I was going out. And I, well, I don't have any credit left on mine.' His face reddened again.

'Of course.' She handed him her mobile.

He punched in the number and waited. 'Hi, Dad, listen . . . yes, I know . . . Mum'll just have to do it herself . . . No, Dad, I can't do it now . . . I'm helping this lady from the police . . . We're working on a case . . .' He rolled his eyes at her and got out of the car, still talking.

Hulda remembered the days when she would have been referred to as a girl, not a lady.

While he was gone, Hulda seized the chance to switch on the radio and lie back in her seat for a minute. It had been a long day and it wasn't over yet. But the sky was blue and, after the unpromising start, it had turned into a beautiful sunny evening. Hulda reflected that May was definitely the best time of year in her chilly northern homeland.

After a couple of minutes, Bjartur got back into the car. 'Sorry about that, we can go on now.' He smiled. 'It's only another half an hour or so.'

They had been driving for an hour already, and Hulda was aware of a gnawing hunger: she'd had nothing to eat since this morning's Prins Póló biscuits. She was growing increasingly tired, too. Perhaps she could ask Bjartur to drive on the way back. This journey had better not turn out to be a waste of time. She had made herself a promise that she would abandon the case at the end of the day, but would she be capable of keeping that promise? She still felt uneasy about not being able to contact Albert. She had to speak to him.

Or would she simply obey orders: take all the evidence she had gathered to Magnús and let him finish the case? It would be no joke telling Magnús that she suspected their old colleague Albert of double murder. The lads had a habit of sticking together, and Albert had been accepted as part of the gang, despite being a lawyer rather than a detective.

She cursed under her breath. Maybe she should just drop it. Get this journey over and done with.

She missed Pétur, and suddenly realized that she was almost happy to be retiring after all, that she was excited at the prospect of spending her golden years with him. They could do so many things together, travel around Iceland, abroad even, and enjoy life in each other's company. She would keep up her hiking, now with Pétur, but she could discover new hobbies, too; she was still fit and needed to stay active. She might even take up golf, the hobby of choice for so many of her colleagues. Only sixty-four, and so many things to look forward to; maybe she could try – with Pétur's help – to put the darkness of the past behind her. She hadn't seen things so clearly in a long while.

She was very much looking forward to going home to bed and starting a new life when the sun came up tomorrow: a new life with Pétur.

XXI

After a moment, he groped for one of the head torches on the table and switched it on. Then stared down at her, trying to come to terms with what he had done. He'd been in love with this woman, and now she was lying dead at his feet. He had killed her. It was all so bizarre, somehow.

He would have to salvage what he could of the situation. Think logically. Try to prevent too much blood from spilling on to the floor of the hut.

Think. The most important fact was that no one else had known about their trip. And no one would dream of looking for them here or of searching the hut for evidence of the crime.

It was still dark, which meant he had plenty of time. All he had to do was keep a cool head and act methodically.

It was the first time he had ever killed anyone, and, in truth, it had been disturbingly easy.

XXII

'I think we're on the right track,' Bjartur said. 'This is the valley Elena mentioned, though I'm not aware of any buildings here. But then it's a long time since I last visited the area.' Then he added: 'Are you sure we should go here? I'm not really used to – you know, tracking a killer . . .'

'We can't turn back now we've travelled this far,' Hulda said. 'It'll be OK. I don't for a minute believe we're in any danger. Is this the right direction? Do we keep heading up the valley?' The road had dwindled to a gravel track, its surface deteriorating with every kilometre.

'Yes, that's right.'

As they continued their juddering progress up the valley, Hulda spared the odd fleeting thought for her Skoda, anxious that it might not be able to cope with the potholes, but other worries were crowding for attention in her head: the death at the hospital; the mother on her way to jail; the potential repercussions of this tragic incident for Hulda herself; the way she had ruined everything in one spectacularly horrible week. Elena was increasingly fading from view, pushed out by these other concerns.

It was a beautiful evening, the sun hung low in an almost cloudless sky, and a group of newly planted saplings cast long shadows over the pale grass of the valley. The slopes had yet to turn green, as spring was not as advanced up here as it was down in the city. For a moment, looking round at the wide-open spaces and boundless blue sky, Hulda experienced a feeling of freedom, that her potential was limitless. But then her tiredness reasserted itself and she would have given anything to be enjoying the weather somewhere else: preferably looking out over Pétur's garden in Fossvogur.

'Perhaps we should call it a day,' she muttered, after five more minutes of bone-shaking progress.

'Yeah, I agree,' said Bjartur. 'There's a better turning spot just a hundred metres or so up ahead.' Next moment, he shouted triumphantly: 'House! Look, there's a building. That's new. It wasn't there the last time I came up here.'

Hulda slowed down and followed Bjartur's pointing finger.

'Shall we check it out?' he suggested. 'I bet it's the house Elena was referring to.'

'Absolutely,' Hulda said.

'House' was a bit of an exaggeration. As they drew nearer, it was revealed as a primitive hut or cabin, next to what appeared to be a building site. Although there was no sign of anyone at work, it was clear that these were the foundations for a larger house that was currently under construction. Hulda parked in front of the hut and, from habit, scanned the surroundings carefully before getting out of the car. It would have been impossible for anyone to hide out here in this open, grassy landscape, in the light summer night. There weren't even any rocks. The only potential hiding place was the hut itself.

Hulda met Bjartur's eye. 'There's nothing to see here.'

'Shouldn't we at least take a quick look inside?' he asked.

'We don't have a warrant,' she objected, though she felt sorely tempted to flout the rules. After all, what had she got to lose? Especially now they'd come all this way.

'We could look in through the windows,' Bjartur suggested.

Hulda shrugged. She could hardly stop him.

He made a circuit of the little hut, peering in at the windows. Then, without warning, he tried the handle and the door opened. 'It's unlocked,' he called, and before she could react he had stepped inside.

'Oh, what the hell,' Hulda muttered, and set off unhurriedly after him, reflecting that, even if someone found out, she couldn't be sacked twice.

As she entered the hut she could feel her heart beating faster in anticipation, the old adrenaline pulsing through her veins, and with that her brain suddenly seemed to awake from its torpor: Amena's elusive comment, which had been niggling at her for the last couple of hours, came to her in a flash. The evening before she died, Elena had sat talking for ages on the phone in the hostel lobby. But Hulda now clearly recalled the receptionist telling her that international calls were blocked. And Elena only really spoke Russian. Was it possible that she had been talking to Bjartur?

Bjartur.

Where had he got to? She couldn't see him anywhere inside the tiny hut. Before she could look round, she felt a heavy blow land on her head.

XXIII

It took a while to clean the hut, hampered by the dark, and even then it was clear that he would have to come back as soon as possible with stronger products to try to obliterate any remaining traces. He felt oddly detached, as though some other man had hit the woman over the head with the axe and he was saddled with the job of cleaning up after him. In a way, he felt sorry for Katja, yet at the same time he was furious with her for behaving so foolishly. She didn't deserve to die but, in the circumstances, his reaction had been the only one possible.

A glance at the hut's guestbook confirmed that days, even weeks, tended to pass between visits at this time of year, so he should be able to get away with it if he came straight back this evening.

But right now, the priority was to dispose of the body.

He had zipped it into her sleeping bag then dragged it all the way back to his car, confident that the falling snow would cover his tracks fairly quickly. In the dark hours before dawn, in the dead of winter, far from civilization, he was confident of being able to act without being seen or interrupted. The problem was how to get rid of the body. All the solutions he came up with would entail a risk, some greater than others.

In the end, he made up his mind to drive into the interior, heading for the nearest ice cap. He knew of a belt of crevasses that would be ideal for his purpose. The final stretch was inaccessible by car, but in these freezing, snowy conditions it would be safe to cover it on skis. Such a thing would never have been possible in summer, when the glaciers were crawling with tourists, but at this time of year it was worth the risk. So that's where he was going now, and that's where he would make sure that Katja disappeared for ever.

XXIV

For too long, Hulda had closed her eyes to the truth. She had lived with the devastating consequences of that fact for quarter of a century now. She wasn't sure when she had realized what was going on but, by then, it was already too late. This she blamed partly on denial, partly on her blindness to what was going on right under her nose. The hideous irony of it didn't escape her. After all, she had prided herself on her powers of perception, regarded herself as one of the best detectives on the force, precisely because nothing ever got past her, because she had a knack of seeing through all the lies and deception well ahead of her colleagues.

But when the crime was being committed in her own home, she hadn't noticed a thing.

Or hadn't wanted to notice.

Confronting the fact had been almost unthinkable. She had been in love with Jón for most of her adult life; they had married young, and he had always treated her well, been an honest, trustworthy husband. Their love had blossomed, at least for a time, and it had been true love; she remembered the first year of their courtship, she had been swept off her feet by this handsome, suave man, who seemed so urbane and worldly. So it had been all too easy to overlook certain clues, to convince herself that they meant something different.

They had both been so happy when Dimma was born, such proud parents. But when she turned ten, their daughter's behaviour had undergone a change and she'd become moody and withdrawn, suffering from bouts of depression. Yet still Hulda hadn't twigged. She had allowed herself the luxury of living in ignorance, persuading herself that the cause couldn't lie at home.

Naturally, Hulda had tried to talk to her daughter. She'd asked her why she was feeling so bad, what had happened to upset her, but Dimma had proved stubbornly uncommunicative, refusing to provide any answers, determined to suffer in silence. In moments of desperation, Hulda even wondered, ridiculously, if they had somehow brought this on themselves by choosing such an unusual name for their daughter: Dimma, meaning 'darkness'. It was as if they had condemned her from birth, although they had only chosen the name for its nice, poetic ring. In her saner moments, she dismissed such thoughts as foolish nonsense.

In hindsight, Hulda regretted that she hadn't put more pressure on Dimma, that she hadn't demanded an answer. The child had been trapped in a desperate dilemma, sinking further into the abyss with every day that passed.

In those last few weeks before Dimma killed herself at

only thirteen years old, Hulda's sleep had been restless, as though she had a foreboding of disaster. Yet even so, she had failed to intervene with the forcefulness that might have saved Dimma's life.

The moment Dimma died, the moment she saw Jón's reaction, the truth had come crashing home to her. She didn't even need to ask. Her whole world had been transformed overnight. But for some reason, they had continued to put on an act, living in the same house, presenting a united face to the outside world, though their marriage had ended in that moment. Perhaps she had wanted to avoid the fallout from a direct confrontation with Jón, fearing that his terrible crime would somehow taint her by association. That tongues would wag, whispering that she must have known, that she could have done something, could have stopped him and saved her daughter. Saved Dimma's life. The most unbearable part was that there might have been a grain of truth in those accusations. So she hadn't said a word to the man she had once cared for. Never asked him what he had done to the daughter she had loved more than life itself. Didn't want to know how long the abuse had been going on. But one thing she was sure of: Dimma's suicide had been a direct consequence of that abuse. Dimma may have taken her own life, but Jón bore full responsibility for her death.

Besides, Hulda couldn't bear to listen to any of the details, to picture any of the sickening acts to which he had subjected her daughter.

When Dimma died, something had died inside Hulda, too. In the depths of her suffering, when the grief felt unendurable, on the days when she felt to blame for what had happened – countless days, countless sleepless nights – the only thing that had kept her going was her violent hatred of Jón.

They never spoke of their daughter again, never mentioned her name to each other. Hulda couldn't bring herself to speak about her in the presence of this stranger, this . . . monster. And Jón had had the sense never to refer to Dimma again in Hulda's hearing.

XXV

It took Hulda a while to come to her senses. At first, she couldn't remember what had happened, where she was or who was with her. But when the events finally came back to her and she tried to open her eyes, she became aware of a blinding headache.

She was lying somewhere. Overhead was the light night sky, but also . . . was that earth? Where was she?

She closed her eyes again. Christ, her head was splitting. He had hit her – Bjartur had hit her on the head. Opening her eyes a crack, she discovered, to her disbelieving horror, that she was lying in the foundation trench of the building site in the valley.

And then she caught sight of Bjartur holding a spade.

She tried to scream but, as soon as she opened her mouth, it filled with sand. Spitting it out, she managed to croak through parched lips: 'What are you doing?'

Bjartur smiled, looking spookily calm.

'To be honest, I wasn't expecting you to come round,' he said slowly. 'You can scream all you like: we're alone here. The property belongs to a friend of mine. I've been helping him build a holiday cottage here.'

She struggled in vain to sit up.

'I tied you up, anyway, just to be on the safe side,' he added, chucking a heaped spadeful of soil on top of her. The earth landed heavily on her face and chest. She had instinctively closed her eyes, and when she opened them again the grit made them sting.

'What the hell do you think you're doing?' she swore, her fear momentarily giving way to incredulous anger.

'Burying you in the foundations, making sure you disappear. Under the cottage.'

Her mind working frantically, Hulda played for time. 'Can I . . . can I have a drink of water?'

'Water?'

He thought about it. 'No, there's no point. It's your own fault, you know. You should *never* have come nosing around, questioning me about Katja. No one had spotted the connection between Katja and Elena . . . and me. I can't take any chances. Surely you must see that?'

'You mean you're going to kill me?'

'I . . . I'm going to bury you. After that, presumably, you'll die.'

Her heart crashing against her ribcage, Hulda made a frenzied attempt to break free but found she could only wriggle from side to side. Bjartur rested the tip of the spade on her chest, pressing hard. 'Lie still!'

'Is this . . . Is this how you got rid of Katja?' Hulda asked. Anything to keep him talking.

'Sort of. But she's . . . lying somewhere else.'

'Where?'

'I don't think that's any of your business. On the other hand, I don't suppose you'll be able to tell anyone. She's in a colder place than you.' He grinned. 'She took a trip to the countryside with me as well, though the circumstances were very different. You see, I was in love with her and she knew it. I thought the trip was the beginning of a relationship, but she thought differently, and . . . well, what's done is done.'

Hulda fought to steady her breathing, to resist the rising tide of panic so she could use her brain. She must be able to think her way out of this. Talk him round. To do that, she needed to win time, engage him in conversation. Anything to keep her mind off the prospect of being buried alive.

'You murdered Elena, didn't you?' she said, mastering her voice. 'You two had a long phone conversation the evening before she died. You never mentioned that.'

'Elena. She worked it out,' Bjartur said. He had resumed shovelling earth on top of Hulda but now paused again, resting the tip of his spade on the ground for a moment. 'Elena was the only person who knew that Katja and I were close friends. She wouldn't stop pestering me about what had happened to her. At first, I lied and said I'd helped Katja give the authorities the slip; that she was hiding out in the countryside. But Elena kept nagging at me to let her see Katja. Then she rang me the evening she . . . she died. She was threatening to go to the police. I tried to convince her not to. I had to stop her, you must see that?'

Hulda nodded.

'I invited her for a walk down by the sea later that evening. She had no reason to be afraid of me.'

XXVI

'I've got to see Katja!' Elena said over the phone. 'I've got to!'

'Well, you can't,' Bjartur said. He was sitting in his garage, or rather his parents' garage. It had been a challenging month: too few jobs coming in, and he'd been feeling too listless to work on his own writing. The incident in the highlands was preying on his mind. He kept replaying it in his head, the moment when he had been forced to kill the woman he loved. Katja, who had come to the country as an asylum-seeker; who he had met when he was hired to interpret for her. They'd hit it off so well from the start, or so he'd believed. And she was so beautiful. As Katja didn't speak a word of English, she had often turned to him for help and, sometimes, they had ended up chatting all evening. They shared an interest in nature and Russian literature. He'd never found it easy to talk to women, not Icelandic women, anyway, and now that he was over forty he had pretty much resigned himself to being single, but then Katja had entered his life. He had fantasized about marrying her, which would automatically entitle her to a residence permit. Maybe he could move out of his parents' place, or pack them off to an old people's home and move into their house with Katja. In his imagination, he had already planned their future together and was just waiting for the right moment, confident that Katja felt the same. That she loved him. Then she had casually dropped into conversation that she'd like to get out of town some time. He had immediately taken her at her word, aware that this was his chance. He would take her into the interior, where they could stay in a mountain hut. And there, when it was just the two of them, cut off from the outside world, their relationship would begin.

But things had turned out quite differently. He'd ended up having to kill her. Of course, he hadn't wanted to but then, sometimes, you didn't have a choice. Like in Elena's case; he'd been forced to kill her as well. She was always asking about Katja, and he had to lie, claim that he'd helped her go into hiding; that Katja had heard she was unlikely to get her residence permit and panicked. Of course, this wasn't true either, but he'd had to come up with a plausible reason for why she should have run away. Elena hadn't questioned the story.

He had been praying that Elena would be deported from Iceland soon so he would never have to see her again. And that Katja's fate would never come to light. The police had carried out a search for her, but no one had been aware of their trip to the mountains and no one — with the exception of Elena — knew that he and Katja had got on so well. Got on so well, that is, until the night in the hut.

But then came the day of Elena's phone call. She had been told, as far as she could grasp with her limited English, that her application had been accepted. Her call to tell him the news had thrown him into a blind panic: she wanted to see Katja, to tell her the good news and persuade her to give herself up so they could start a new life together in Iceland.

'I've got to see her,' Elena insisted. 'And you're the only person *who can help. Just tell me where she is – I won't tell anyone. I just want to see her, talk to her.'*

'We can't take the risk,' he said.

There was a silence at the other end.

'Then I'm going to the police,' Elena announced.

'The police?'

'Yes. I'm going to tell them you helped her run away. If the police question you, you'll have to tell them the truth. And then she might have a chance, don't you understand? A chance to get an actual residence permit. But she's got to give herself up first!'

There was another silence. They had been on the phone so long that Bjartur's nerves were in tatters. He was worn out with the strain of having to lie. And now he was afraid, too.

He couldn't go to prison. He couldn't. The murder mustn't come to light. Her body was lying safely hidden at the bottom of a crevasse and he had done his best to scrub away any incriminating evidence from the hut. Besides, no one, not a soul, had a clue that they'd been there. He'd got away with it, or so he had thought, until that bitch Elena had decided to ruin everything.

'OK,' he said at last.

'OK?' repeated Elena, audibly astonished. 'You want me to go to the police?'

'No, I'll tell you where she is. Or . . . wouldn't you rather come with me this evening and see her in person?'

'What? Seriously? Yes, of course I would.'

'I'm sure it'll be all right. It's a big day, exciting news . . . I'll take you there.'

As he spoke, the wheels in his mind were busy turning, working out the perfect spot: the isolated little cove at Flekkuvík, about half-way between Reykjavík and Keflavík. It was an area he knew well;

through his work as a guide, he was familiar with much of his country's geography, either from first-hand experience or reading about it in books. The advantage of this particular cove was that, although only quarter of an hour's drive from Njardvík, it wasn't overlooked by any houses or the road. They were guaranteed to be the only people around since it wasn't even accessible by car: they would have to get out and walk the last few hundred yards.

'Can you come and pick me up?' Elena asked.

'Hmm . . . not from the hostel. I can't take the risk of being seen — because of Katja being in hiding, you understand.' He mentioned a shop within walking distance of the hostel and asked Elena to meet him there.

'It's such a long way,' Elena whined, her teeth chattering from the cold. Although there was no snow on the ground, the weather was freezing and she wasn't adequately dressed. Still, it couldn't be helped. Bjartur led the way along the path to the cove. Ahead loomed a couple of buildings, hard to make out in the gloom.

'She's in that house over there, the one closer to the sea,' he said at last.

'Seriously? Katja's there?'

'No one would think of looking for her here.'

'Unbelievable. You mean she's been here all the time?'

'She was staying with me to begin with,' Bjartur said, allowing a little warmth to steal into his voice. For a moment, he almost believed it himself, recalling his fantasy about marrying her and taking her to live in his house. 'But it was too risky,' he went on. 'I've got my elderly parents living with me. They'd have found out sooner or later.'

'I see,' Elena said.

He couldn't read her expression in the darkness. Was she convinced?

'I'm sure she'll be eligible for a residence permit, like me,' Elena continued after a moment. 'Our situations aren't that different.'

'Right,' said Bjartur. 'Right.'

'But . . . it's a pity she had to run away like that. Was it your idea?' Her voice was accusatory.

'Mine? Of course not.' Bjartur adopted an injured tone. 'I did my best to talk her out of it.'

'Does she know? That we're coming, I mean?'

'No. She hasn't got a phone.'

Elena was silent.

Only as they approached the houses did she speak again.

'You know what, this doesn't feel right, Bjartur. No one could live here. There's no glass in the windows. These buildings are empty.'

'Don't be silly. I assure you she's here.'

Elena turned to look at him, and now he could see that her eyes were narrowed with suspicion.

'Are you lying to me?'

Alone with him in the cold and dark, she seemed suddenly tense with fear.

Bjartur halted. There was hardly a breath of wind, and the murmur of the waves was mesmerizing. He studied her. She couldn't escape now.

'Are you lying? Why are you lying?' Her voice rose, sounding high and strained: 'Where's Katja?'

She began to back away from him. Bjartur didn't move.

Then she turned and fled into the night.

It didn't take him long to catch up. When he did, he hurled her to the ground, grabbed a nearby stone and bashed her on the head, knocking her out. Was she dead? Probably not. He thought he could detect a pulse.

Bjartur lifted her up and carted her limp body down to the cove, stumbling once or twice on the rocks in the darkness. Then he laid Elena carefully on her front, with her head in the salt water, and held her down.

XXVII

'You mean there was nothing in the papers I brought you?' Hulda asked, her mind working furiously, determined to do everything in her power to keep the conversation going.

Bjartur laughed. 'Nothing of interest. Obviously, I had to think fast when you mentioned Katja; find some excuse to lure you out of town. I had to get rid of you. There's no alternative.'

Hulda cursed silently. This had turned into the day from hell. All her mistakes came back to haunt her: Emma's confession, the man murdered in hospital, Áki's arrest. She should never have got out of bed. Normally, she told herself, she'd have been far quicker to sense the danger she was in, but worry had blunted her instincts.

'Please, give me some water,' Hulda gasped, though it went against the grain to ask this man for anything.

'Later,' he said, but she wasn't sure he meant it.

'Were they both working as prostitutes?' she asked.

Bjartur burst out laughing. 'Of course not. Neither of

them was. They were good girls, especially Katja – she was lovely.'

'But . . .' Only now, far too late, did Hulda understand how Bjartur had misled her, set her on the wrong path at the very outset of the investigation.

'I was so thrown when you appeared on my doorstep,' he went on. 'I'd put the whole thing behind me; thought the case was closed ages ago. All I could think was to find some way of deflecting your attention from me. Then I had a brainwave: I'd tell you Elena had been on the game. And it worked pretty well, didn't it? Had you fooled.'

Hulda blinked, her eyes full of dirt. When they cleared, she saw that Bjartur was smiling, absently.

She could feel the terror clutching at her heart, but she mustn't let it paralyse her. For a moment, she was a child again, locked in the naughty cupboard by her grandmother.

Closing her eyes briefly, she concentrated on the birdsong. Surely somebody would help her. Even though it was past midnight, there must be someone about. Or perhaps Bjartur would change his mind, perhaps he was only trying to frighten her . . . Her hopes ebbed away with every second that passed.

'You won't get away with this,' she said at last, but it sounded unconvincing, even to her own ears.

'I've already got away with two murders. I'm getting to be quite an old hand. And I'll make sure you're never found. We're laying the concrete foundation this week.'

'But . . .' Her mind flew to her mobile. It must be

possible to track her whereabouts, find out where she'd been, even if it was too late to save her.

Once again, Bjartur seemed to read her mind.

'I dealt with your phone hours ago. Remember when you lent it to me and I pretended to call my dad? I took out the battery.'

'There's still my car.'

'That's a bit more of a headache, I grant you, but I'll dispose of it. Drive it off a cliff into the sea then make my way back to town somehow. Anyway, no one'll be interested in my movements, since I've never been a suspect in this case. Don't worry, I'll get away with it.'

He resumed his shovelling.

XXVIII

The advantage of darkness is that there are no shadows.

Hulda closed her eyes.

She decided to stop struggling. Give up the fight.

The suffocating sense of claustrophobia was horrific, indescribable, yet, oddly, she felt a kind of peace descending on her, once she had resigned herself to the inevitable, to the realization that no one was coming to her rescue now, that these were her final moments of life. She would never have to endure the humiliation of being prosecuted for professional misconduct. In the event of her death, Magnús would drop the proceedings against her, she was sure of that. Her thoughts flew to Pétur. He would be waiting for her. Perhaps he had been trying to call her. And he would have to wait for ever.

Her face was almost completely covered with earth now.

Above all, death offered a merciful way out: an end to the nightmares. The long-desired absolution. Peace. For the last twenty years and more, Hulda had been trying to atone for what she had done, for the act that weighed so heavily on her soul, by showing understanding and sympathy to the guilty. At times, this had led her to cross a line, as in the case of Emma. The woman had committed a crime, driven her car into a paedophile, but Hulda had understood her all too well.

She didn't know how long she had left. Perhaps only a few brief seconds.

At that moment, she almost wished she believed in a higher power. She had gone to church regularly with her grandparents as a child, but later, after the death of her daughter, the last vestiges of her faith had deserted her.

Her thoughts returned to Jón and Dimma.

Once, she had loved no one in the world as much as those two, her husband and her daughter. But when she found out that Jón had been subjecting Dimma to unspeakable cruelty, her love had been transformed into hate. In one fell swoop, she had lost them both: Dimma had taken her own life; Jón had been transformed into a monster. Her hatred had grown and intensified every day, swelling into a vast, uncontrollable rage. What he had done could never be forgiven, yet he was alive and Dimma was not. Every time Hulda saw him, she thought of Dimma. Her daughter was dead, she had failed her, and yet she was flooded with a mother's love more powerful even than when Dimma had been alive.

She had to erase Jón from her life. But divorcing him wouldn't be enough and she had no desire to drag the family through a public sexual-abuse inquiry. That was out of the question. No, she wanted everything to remain fine on the surface, but Jón had to go, and he had to pay for his hideous crimes.

In the event, it had proved quite easy.

Jón had a heart condition, but he could have lived to a ripe old age with the right medication.

Hulda had replaced his pills with a useless substitute, and then waited, hoping the change would have some effect, that he would – one fine day – simply fall asleep and never wake up again.

Of course, she knew what she was doing was wrong. Not only wrong but murder, pure and simple. Yet she pushed these feelings away, focusing on the job at hand, on getting rid of Jón. And hopefully finding a little peace. The desire for justice was overwhelming; she had to avenge her daughter's death. But, more than that, she couldn't bear the thought of Jón being allowed to live any longer.

After the plan came to her, she never really had any second thoughts. They came later; too late.

In the end, she had had enough of waiting. One day, she came home for lunch, knowing that Jón would be there. She deliberately picked a fight with him and kept at it mercilessly, working Jón up into such a state that he suffered a massive cardiac arrest.

He fell to the living-room floor, unable to speak, unable to cry out, but he was still alive. He looked at her, his eyes pleading. He couldn't know what she'd done, and Hulda felt no urge to explain. She just stood there and watched him die, thinking of Dimma. She felt nothing; no regrets, but no pleasure either. And then, when he was finally gone, there was a feeling of relief, that it was over at last.

Hulda knew she could finally move on. Nothing would ever be normal again, of course, but she had done what she had to do.

She had killed a man who had committed a crime worse than murder.

She left him on the floor and went back to work.

Later, she came home, 'found' the body and called an ambulance. And that was that.

A man with a weak heart drops dead before his time. Nothing unusual about that. His daughter had killed herself not long before; it had all proved a great strain. There wasn't a whisper of suspicion about the real reason for Dimma's suicide, let alone that there might have been anything unnatural about Jón's death. Everyone's sympathies lay with his wife, who was, moreover, a police officer. Of course, there was no inquest. And, of course, she got away with it, but hardly a night had passed since then when Jón hadn't revisited her in her dreams. She had committed murder and got away with it, but discovered that she couldn't live with the fact.

So perhaps it was a fitting punishment, she thought, that her life should end in this cruel manner.

Hulda tried not to panic, though the earth was blocking her airways now, making her choke. She waited for the inevitable, thinking of her daughter. Of course, Dimma had never left her thoughts, not really, but now she could see her face clearly and was flooded with boundless love, mingled with terrible guilt.

Dimma . . .

Bjartur seemed to have paused in his shovelling. To catch his breath, perhaps. Or had she maybe spoken her daughter's name aloud and momentarily disconcerted him?

Then he began again.

The birds sang.

They didn't know it was night.

Epilogue

'It's gratifying to see so many of you gathered here, on this beautiful day, as we pay our last respects to Hulda Hermannsdóttir,' the priest said. 'Of course, this is not a funeral as such, since, as we're all aware, Hulda has not yet been found. We pray with all our hearts that she's out there somewhere, still with us, still enjoying life; that she simply left, for reasons of her own. So perhaps we should look on this occasion rather as an opportunity to celebrate Hulda's life, although it is of course a sad occasion in many respects. No one here knows exactly what happened on Hulda's last day at work or why she should have vanished without trace, just as she was about to embark on a long and happy retirement, the reward for all her years of dedicated service with the police. It goes without saying that not everyone welcomes that milestone: some dread the day; others can't wait. We don't know how Hulda felt about retirement or what was going through her mind on that last day, nor do we know where her body is resting now, but one thing we can be sure of, and that is that she can rest there, reconciled to God and her fellow men.

'Hulda enjoyed a distinguished career with the police, rising rapidly through the ranks and commanding the respect of junior and senior officers alike. Much of that career was dedicated to investigating serious crimes, to ensure the peace and security of her fellow citizens. In recent years, she was involved in solving many of our most high-profile cases, often at the forefront of the inquiry, at other times working behind the scenes, eschewing the limelight with characteristic modesty.

'Many of Hulda's colleagues went beyond the call of duty in their efforts to search for her this spring, despite the almost total lack of indications as to where she had gone missing. I know that Hulda would have been deeply moved by the selfless generosity of their endeavours, which is testimony to the affection in which they held her. Her friends refused to give up their ceaseless hunt until all hope of finding her was lost. Much of their time was spent combing the highlands where, one could say, Hulda had been on home ground. As you are all no doubt aware, Hulda's greatest passion was for walking in the mountains: in her own words, she was a real mountain goat. I've lost count of the peaks she climbed – she'd probably lost count of them herself. Let us picture her, then, on the eve of her retirement, striding up one of her favourite mountains to mark the occasion, a journey that turned out to be her last. And let us take comfort from the thought that she now rests in the heart of the Icelandic wilderness that she so loved.

'Hulda spent the first two years of her life at a

children's home in Reykjavík, due to difficult family circumstances. Such things were not unusual in those days,
but she was well cared for by the dedicated staff. At the
age of two, she went to live with her mother and, later,
they moved in with her maternal grandparents, to make
one big family, and Hulda always maintained a strong,
close bond with her mother, grandfather and grandmother. This happy, loving childhood served Hulda well
later in life: she had an open, sunny disposition and got
on well with everyone. Hulda never met her father, who
was an American.

'But there were two people above all who occupied the
most important place in Hulda's heart. One was her husband, Jón, whom she met young and married after only a
short acquaintance; a happy decision; they have been
described as true soul-mates. Hulda and Jón stuck
together through thick and thin, shared many interests
and complemented one another, as good companions
should. Friends testify to the fact that they never
exchanged a cross word. They made their home by the
sea on Álftanes, still a rural area in those days, and perhaps it was there that Hulda's passion for the Icelandic
landscape was first kindled.

'It was also there that the apple of their eye, their
daughter, Dimma, was born. Dimma was popular at
school and a model pupil, a little girl of great promise,
and, unsurprisingly, Hulda and Jón were enormously
proud of her. So her tragic death in her early teens came
as a devastating blow to her parents. They coped with
stoicism and courage, inseparable as ever, no doubt

drawing great comfort from one another. They continued to live on Álftanes and eventually returned to work: Hulda to the police, Jón to his job in investment. Then, two years later, Hulda also lost Jón, the love of her life. He had been diagnosed with a heart condition several years earlier, but no one had expected him to die so young. Once again, Hulda was called on to cope with a dreadful shock and responded with indomitable courage, getting back on her feet, tackling life and continuing to make her mark in a demanding profession.

'Hulda never forgot Jón or Dimma. And, as we are aware, she always remained true to her Christian faith, in the conviction that she would be reunited with her loved ones in the next life. For all of us who miss Hulda so keenly, there is comfort in the knowledge that she is resting now in the arms of Jón and Dimma, whom she loved more than life itself.

'God bless the memory of Hulda Hermannsdóttir.'

Hulda will return in

THE ISLAND

Read on for the first chapter
from the second gripping instalment
in the HIDDEN ICELAND trilogy,
set twenty-five years earlier.

COMING 2019

Prelude

Kópavogur, 1988

The babysitter was late.

The couple hardly ever went out in the evening, so they had been careful to check her availability well in advance. She had babysat for them a few times before and lived in the next street, but apart from that they didn't know much about her. Or her family either, though they knew her mother to speak to when they ran into her in the neighbourhood. Their seven-year-old daughter looked up to the girl, who was twenty-one and seemed very grown up and glamorous to her. She was always talking about what fun she was, what pretty clothes she wore, what exciting bedtime stories she told, and so on. Their daughter's eagerness to have her round to babysit made the couple feel less guilty about accepting the invitation; they felt reassured that their little girl would not only be in good hands but would enjoy herself, too. They had arranged for the girl to babysit from six until

313

midnight, but it was already past six, getting on for half past in fact, and the dinner was due to start at seven. The husband wanted to ring and ask what had happened to her, but his wife was reluctant to make a fuss: she'd turn up.

It was a Saturday evening in March and the atmosphere had been one of happy anticipation until the babysitter failed to turn up on time. The couple were looking forward to an entertaining evening with the wife's colleagues from the ministry and their daughter was excited about spending the evening watching films with the babysitter. They didn't own a VCR, but, as it was a special occasion, father and daughter had gone down to the local video store and rented a machine and three tapes, and the little girl had permission to stay up as late as she liked, until she ran out of steam.

It was just after half six when the doorbell finally rang. The family lived on the second floor of a small block of flats in Kópavogur, the town immediately to the south of Reykjavík. The mother picked up the entryphone. It was the babysitter at last. She appeared at their door a few moments later, soaked to the skin, and explained that she'd walked over. It was raining so hard it was like having a bucket emptied over your head. She apologized, embarrassed, for being so late.

The couple waved away her apologies, determined not to let the delay spoil their evening. They thanked her for standing in for them, reminded her of the main house rules and asked if she knew how to work a video recorder, at which point their daughter broke in to say she didn't need any help. Clearly, she could hardly wait to bundle her parents out of the door so the video fest could begin, though the family invariably spent their Saturday evenings glued to the television as it was.

In spite of the taxi waiting outside, the couple couldn't tear themselves away. They just weren't used to leaving their daughter. 'Don't worry,' the babysitter said at last, 'I'll take good care of her.' She looked comfortingly reliable as she said this, and as she'd always done a good job of looking after their daughter in the past, it was in a fairly cheerful frame of mind that they finally headed out into the downpour.

The evening went well, but as it wore on, the mother began to feel increasingly anxious about their daughter.

'Don't be silly,' said her husband. 'I bet she's having a whale of a time.' Glancing at his watch, he added, 'She'll be on her second or third film by now, and they'll have polished off all the ice cream.'

'Do you think they'd let me use the phone at the front desk?' asked his wife.

'It's a bit late to ring them now, isn't it? She may have dropped off in front of the TV.'

In the end, they set off home a little earlier than planned, just after eleven. The three-course dinner was over by then, and to be honest it had been a bit underwhelming. The main course, which was lamb, had been bland at best. After dinner, people had piled on to the dance floor. To begin with, the DJ had played popular oldies, but then he moved on to more recent chart hits, which weren't really the couple's sort of thing, although they still liked to think of themselves as young; after all, they weren't middle-aged yet.

They rode home in silence, the rain streaming down the taxi's windows. The truth was they weren't really party people; they were too fond of their creature comforts at home, and the evening had tired them out, though they hadn't drunk much, just a glass of red wine with dinner.

As they got out of the taxi, the wife remarked that she hoped their daughter was asleep so they could both crawl straight into bed.

They climbed the stairs unhurriedly and opened the door instead of ringing the bell, for fear of disturbing the child.

But she wasn't asleep, as it turned out. She came running to greet them, threw her arms around them and hugged them unusually tightly. To their surprise, she seemed wide awake; they'd have expected her to be nodding off by now.

'You're full of beans,' said her father, smiling at her.

'I'm so glad you're home,' said the little girl. There was an odd look in her eye; something was wrong, though it was hard to define what it was.

The babysitter emerged from the sitting room and smiled sweetly at them.

'How did it go?' asked the mother.

'Really well,' the babysitter replied, 'Your daughter's such a good girl. We watched two videos.'

'Thanks so much for coming; I don't know what we'd have done without you.'

The father took his wallet from his jacket, counted out some notes and handed them to her. 'Is that right?'

She counted the money herself, then nodded. 'Yes, perfect.'

After she'd left, the father turned to their daughter.

'Aren't you tired, sweetheart?'

'Yes, maybe a little. But could we watch just a bit more?'

Her father shook his head, saying kindly, 'Sorry, it's awfully late.'

'Oh, please. I don't want to go to bed yet,' said the little girl, sounding on the verge of tears.

'OK, OK.' He ushered her into the sitting room. The TV schedule was over for the evening, but he turned on the video machine and inserted a new cassette.

Then he joined her on the sofa and they waited for the film to begin.

'Didn't you have a nice time together?' he asked, warily.

'Yes ... yes, it was fine,' she said, not very convincingly.

'She was ... kind to you, wasn't she?'

'Yes,' answered the child. 'Yes, they were both kind.'

Her father was wrong-footed. 'What do you mean *both*?' he asked.

'There were two of them.'

Turning round to look at her, he asked again, gently: 'What do you mean by *them*?'

'There were two of them.'

'Did one of her friends come round?'

There was a brief pause before the girl answered. Seeing the fear in her eyes, he gave an involuntary shiver.

'No. But it was kind of weird, Daddy . . .'